WELCOME BACK, MISTER STARNES

MORGAN CROSSROADS SERIES - BOOK 2

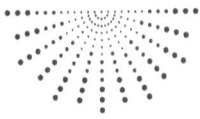

TOM BUFORD

Welcome Back, Mister Starnes
Morgan Crossroads Series, Book 2

———

Paperback ISBN 978-0-9708103-9-7

Quiet Place Media
P. O. Box 2226
Castalian Springs, TN 37031

Join Tom's mailing list at
https://tombuford.com/**subscribe**/

Welcome Back Mister Starnes is a work of fiction. The characters, incidents and dialogue are drawn from the author's imagination and are not to be construed as real. Morgan Crossroads and Whipper County, Alabama exist only in the mind of the author and in the pages of *Welcome Back Mister Starnes* and other books in The Morgan Crossroads series of fun fiction.

Any similarity between places or characters in this book and places or people, living or dead, that may exist somewhere in the world is purely coincidental. If the places and characters in this story remind you of a place you've wished you lived or a person you've wished you'd known, that's good. That means Tom did his job.

CHAPTER ONE

It was a big deal. Lucy's Cafe was ablaze with reds and yellows and blues. Three large tables stood in the rear corner, each covered with a linen tablecloth and silk lace overlay. Table settings were complete with precisely placed fine china, crystal stemware, and silver flatware laid out on colored place mats and decorated with eye-popping hand-made origami flowers.

Stella, the owner of Lucy's Cafe had posted a notice on the front door two weeks earlier advising the regulars that she would close the cafe for an unspecified special event on this Thursday evening. That left three choices. They could eat at home. They could drive a few blocks south to the other end of town and eat in their cars at the Dairy Bar. Or they could ride over to Porterville if they wanted to go all out in a restaurant with cloth napkins.

For the first time in its history, the Rosebud Circle of Morgan Crossroads, Alabama was to hold its weekly meeting in the evening instead of Tuesday morning as the ritual had been for thirty years.

To enhance the ambiance, Stella had asked Grumpy from

the welding shop behind the post office to install a dimmer switch for the lights. She had brought in candle stands to add a subtle, but elegant touch to the lighting.

Mary Beth had worked for three days, putting together floral arrangements to accent the candles.

The occasion? Linda Cruz, a young pharmacist, had taken over Crossroads Pharmacy when her uncle retired. She was being welcomed into the Rosebud Circle as the youngest woman ever to become an official member.

The exact criteria for membership in the Rosebud Circle was sketchy since no current members could remember there ever having been any specific requirements. Most men figured the only requirements must be the ability to gossip, eat desserts, and discuss doilies. A woman who could do that could fit right in, the men said.

Truth was, no man had ever attended a Rosebud Circle meeting. Not by invitation, anyway. There was the one time a decade earlier that Ollie Smith became disoriented and wandered into Lucy's Cafe instead of Brown's General Store. He was there to pick up a pouch of chewing tobacco and a pound of bologna. He blamed his unsteady steps and fumbling speech on a case of the crud and the cough syrup he'd been taking to cure it.

There was no minimum age requirement for membership in the Rosebud Circle. But none of the living charter members—Marcella Garrison, Eva Jo Clomper, Polly Brown, or Jewell Crabtree—could name anyone who had been younger than thirty when they joined.

So, it was official. Linda Cruz would be the youngest official member yet. It was exciting to see new life breathed into the group, exciting enough that her induction had inspired the standing members to pull out all the stops for the occasion.

The menu for the evening would include herb-roasted lamb chops, thanks to a special order from Haley's Grocery. There would be a medley of mixed vegetables straight from Jewell Crabtree's garden, fresh green salad, and home-made buttered yeast rolls that no one but Eva Jo could bake. Liz Farrel at the bakery in Porterville volunteered to send over two huge cherry cheesecakes and a chocolate crumb cake for dessert. Stella agreed to provide the venue and all the iced tea and water they could stand.

"Just for the fun of it, why don't we make this a secret meeting? If nothing else, it will be fun watching the men digging around to find out what we're doing," Polly had said.

There was an immediate unanimous vote that no member would tell her husband or family members anything about the meeting.

"You know Henry's gonna go nuts, don't you?" Eva Jo said to Polly.

Polly laughed and waved her hand toward Brown's General Store. "It won't be his first time. He almost did when Marcella brought Edgar home from Texas and announced that she was getting married."

"HAS YOUR WIFE BEEN ACTING AS STRANGE AS MINE?" HENRY Brown asked Ollie Smith when they met on the post office sidewalk.

"Not any more than usual, I reckon. Why?"

"Just curious. Polly's doing hair this week like there's another wedding or something going on. It's almost as bad as when Marcella and Edgar tied the knot."

"Let me guess," Ollie said. "You're having to make your own lunch."

"If I want to eat, I do. She told me this morning that if I needed clean socks before the weekend, I'd have to do my own laundry, too."

Ollie chuckled. "Do you remember how to turn the washing machine on?"

"I know how to wash clothes," Henry huffed. "And according to Polly, I'm licensed to run that old Kirby vacuum cleaner, too."

"She won't tell you what's going on?"

"No. All she'll tell me is that it's a secret, and she'll fill me in on it later, maybe."

"Stella put a sign up on the plate-glass window at Lucy's. Says she's closing up early. Reckon that's got anything to do with it?"

Henry straightened himself. "Watch this," he said, half under his breath. "Here comes Dora Mae. She couldn't keep a secret if there was a million dollar lottery ticket in the deal for her."

"Excuse me." Dora Mae Crawford stepped between Henry and Ollie on her way into the post office.

Henry opened the door for her. "I guess you're going to the whoopee-do tonight."

"What whoopee-do?" she asked. "Is somebody famous coming to town?"

"Not that I know of," Henry said. "Just something that requires a lot of done up hair."

"Like maybe something at Lucy's, tonight?" Ollie said.

"I heard Stella bought some paint brushes," Dora Mae said, then disappeared through the door.

"You got that lottery ticket?" Ollie asked, punching Henry with his elbow.

"What lottery ticket?" asked Grumpy, who ran the post office and the welding shop behind it.

"Where'd you come from?" Ollie asked.

"Up the driveway. I was in the shop and thought I'd take a hike down to Henry's store and get myself an Orange Crush. Who's got a lottery ticket?"

"Nobody," Henry said, choosing not to rehash the story. "We're just trying to figure out what's going on that's got Polly in an uproar. Those women are crowding in to get their hair done up."

Ollie adjusted a strap on his overalls. "Well, I can tell you one thing, guys. It ain't just Polly. Every shop in Morgan Crossroads that's run by a woman is either real busy, or closing early today. And none of them are talking, either."

Henry pulled out his pocket knife and fiddled with it. "Who's closing early beside Stella?"

"Well, I know she is because she put up that sign on the window, plus, she paid me to put in a dimmer switch for her lights," Grumpy said.

"A light dimmer? In Lucy's Cafe?" Ollie said. "Ever since Marcella married Edgar and they moved into that Starnes fellow's house, people sure have been trying to get fancy."

"No, it's got nothing to do with Edgar. I think they've got something planned that they don't want us to know about."

"Who else is shutting down early?" Henry asked.

"Well, I can tell you you ain't gonna order any flowers from Mary Beth until at least Friday. Better not be anybody dying today. That's all I've got to say," Grumpy said.

Ollie said, "That girl at the drugstore told my wife she'd need to pick up her prescriptions before two o'clock. Said she was closing early. Didn't say why, though."

"Eva Jo Clomper told that grandson of hers that she'd pay him twenty dollars to bring her cows in to the barn on Thursday. That's today. Said she had to go somewhere," Henry said.

"Henry, why don't you call Marcella?" Grumpy asked. "Since she's your cousin, she'll probably tell you what's going on."

"I think I'll do that. I sure can't get Polly to tell me. Maybe Marcella will."

Marcella dropped her gardening tools, hurried into the kitchen, and picked up the telephone on what she thought must have been the last ring.

"Henry," she said while scratching her nose with the back of her wrist. "Did you call to offer your gardening skills? I have a spade that will fit your hand perfectly."

"Not quite," Henry said. "Polly's been after me for a month to dig up those holly bushes in the backyard. Say, I heard you ladies are throwing some kind of shindig at Lucy's."

"What shindig might that be?" Marcella asked.

"Polly's been running around here like a chicken with her head missing. The way she's been fixing hair the last day or two, you'd think there's another wedding coming up. I thought I saw you in there this morning."

"Well, you know how she is, Henry. She has no clue what it means to rest. Maybe you need to take her on a vacation sometime. Take her to the Smokies or to North Carolina. I bet she'd have a ball at Biltmore Estate. They say it's beautiful. By the way, she's done my hair at nine o'clock on Thursday morning for twenty years or longer."

"A vacation for us is going out to eat somewhere besides Morgan Crossroads," Henry said. "Anyway, something's going on that nobody wants to tell me about. Grumpy said he installed a dimmer switch on Stella's lights. What does she need that for? People need to see if their food's worth eating."

"Maybe Stella just wants to step up a little, add some romanticism to the atmosphere," Marcella said. "Someone said that new restaurant over in Porterville turns the lights down low at night. I'd bet it's nice, with candles and soft music."

"Yep. And an enormous price to pay for the candles. The higher the price, the more they're afraid for you to see what you're eating. That's what I heard. Anyway, I don't think that's it. Why would Mary Beth stop taking flower orders until Friday? What if somebody dies before then? Can't have a funeral without flowers, you know. Or weddings either, if that's what you all have planned."

"Mary Beth might tell you why she's not taking orders for a day or two. She works hard and deserves a nice break now and then."

"If you say so," Henry said in a defeated voice. "What does Edgar say about the big secret doings?"

"Edgar? He said that he hopes we enjoy ourselves."

"You mean he's not even curious about all this top secret stuff, him being a lawyer and all?"

"I'm sorry but my rose bushes are waiting on me. Are you sure you don't want to try out that spade?"

EDGAR GARRISON PARKED HIS BMW BESIDE GRUMPY'S OLD tow truck at Brown's General Store and joined Henry Brown, Ollie Smith, and Grumpy on the porch.

"Here you go," Ollie said, nudging a rocking chair. "Take a load off your feet, young man."

Edgar lowered himself into the chair. "What I wouldn't give to be a young man again."

Grumpy said, "Hey, you're a lawyer. You're supposed to be good at snooping out what people are hiding."

"Was a lawyer," Edgar said with a wink. "What am I supposed to figure out?"

"These ladies. Every one of them has suddenly gone blank. Can't any of them remember what's going on this evening," Ollie said. "Don't act like they have a clue what you're talking about."

"You can ask one of them why another one of them is acting strange, and she'll just pull on a blank face and stare at you," Grumpy said.

"I tried to find out from Polly and all she told me was to cook my own supper if I wanted to eat," Henry said. "Either that, or go to the Dairy Bar and buy myself a hot dog."

"I heard something about the ladies doing something special, but I have no idea what it might be," Edgar said.

"So she's keeping it a secret from you, too?" Henry said.

"Who is?" Edgar asked.

"Marcella. We've been cousins, and I mean close cousins, for over seventy years, and do you know she acted like nothing?" Henry said.

"How do you act like nothing?" Ollie asked just before he dug another chew from his tobacco pouch.

"You carry on a conversation with questions and answers and all, but you never really talk about the question that you asked in the first place," said Henry.

"What do you want me to do?" Edgar asked.

"Snoop around," Ollie said.

"If Marcella hasn't told you anything by now, I'm betting she won't," Henry said. "At least, she won't volunteer to tell you."

"That's what I say," Grumpy said. "You're gonna have to go on the prowl. Get nosy like that lawyer in the movies. What's his name?"

"Sherlock Holmes," Ollie said.

"Yeah, that's him. Sherlock Holmes."

"I think he was probably a detective, but he'll do in a pinch," Henry said.

Edgar chuckled. "Okay, I'll see what I can do. Where should I start?"

"Well, don't start with Polly. And don't start with Marcella. They're not talking," Henry said.

"Stella likes you pretty good," Grumpy said.

"That right there's a fact," Ollie said. "I've watched how she always brings you the end piece of meatloaf."

Grumpy reached for a new pinch of tobacco. "And somehow, your bread's always warm enough to melt butter."

"She's always topping off your iced tea first thing, too," Ollie said.

"Ollie's right," Henry said. "You could start with Stella, and if that doesn't pan out, you might try Lorraine Haley. Go in there and ask for a ten-pound bag of plain white corn meal. She never has ten-pound bags and she'll try to push one of them five-pounders off on you. Maybe you could argue why you need a ten-pound bag or something else that don't really matter and when you get her so flustered that she has no clue what you're talking about, she might just slip and tell you whatever you want to know."

"What about Eva Jo?" Edgar asked. "She seems to know about things before they happen."

"No good," Grumpy said. "She knows about stuff, and some of it I think she just makes up to throw people off. Do you know she told me one time that she could drive from here to Atlanta in an hour and a half? Why, if she drove that raggedy old pickup truck that fast, all the wheels would fly off of it. The floorboard would fall the rest of the way out. Besides, as far as I know, she's never driven that wreck any further than Huntsville. And," he said, dragging the word out, "she's never even been to Atlanta."

"But she and Marcella are tight like skin on a kneecap," Ollie said. "You'll get exactly nowhere with her."

"No sir," Grumpy said. "If Marcella ain't tellin', Eva Jo ain't either."

HENRY DISAPPEARED THROUGH THE SCREEN DOOR INTO THE store while Ollie and Grumpy watched Edgar's BMW drive away toward Haley's Grocery.

"Lorraine Haley don't have a snowball's chance in July," Ollie wagged his finger down the street. "Not even a little bit."

"No, sir. Edgar's gonna walk in there and turn on that lawyer voice and she won't be able to help herself. You wait and see. I give him fifteen minutes to be right back down here with the whole scoop," Grumpy said.

Henry reappeared with a frosty glass bottle of RC Cola for each of them. "What do you think? Is Lorraine gonna spill the beans?"

"Here's how sure I am of it," Ollie said. "If Edgar comes back down here with no more information than he left with, I'll fire up the grill this evening and throw on a big fat hamburger for any man who wants one."

The men went on guessing what the big secret was for a few minutes.

"Here he comes," Grumpy said, looking at his watch. "Didn't take him long to wear her down, did it?"

"I told you she'd crumble when he got her all flustered," Henry said.

Edgar parked his car and walked to the porch with a grocery bag, which he held out toward Henry. "Here's your cornmeal."

Henry removed a paper bag. "Plain white cornmeal," he read from the label. "Ten pounds."

Grumpy snickered and shot a wad of tobacco juice toward the rusted coffee can next to his rocking chair. "Where'd you come up with that?"

"Lorraine Haley sold it to me, and quite happily, I'd say," Edgar said.

"What did she tell you about the goings on tonight?" Grumpy asked.

"Not a word. She said she'd noticed the sign on the window."

"What's she doing with ten-pound sacks of cornmeal? That's what I want to know. I've been trying for years to buy them from her and she never even offers to order one for me," Henry said. "It's like I've been talking to a brick wall."

"So you couldn't get any information out of her?" Ollie said.

"No, sir. Lorraine was as calm as could be. She said she was getting off early today, though—something about some business to tend to. By the way. I ran into Cecil Grey in the grocery store. It looks as though he'll be playing bachelor tonight, too."

Henry pointed across the porch railing. "Grumpy, you can set that grill up right down there next to the steps. Maybe the wind will blow some of that grilled hamburger smell over their way."

"And then they'll all get jealous," Grumpy said.

Ollie stuffed his pipe with Prince Albert and lit it. "I don't know what those gals are eating over there, but whatever it is, these burgers'll wear them out. Henry, you got any onions?"

Grumpy laughed. "I can just see them now. They'll come streaming out of there with their noses in the air, sniffing, trying to figure where the real cooking is going on."

CHAPTER TWO

Eva Jo Clomper parked her homely-looking pickup truck and stepped out with a fully puffed head of hair, a brand new floral print dress, and her size ten and a half blue low-heeled shoes. She'd dug out the string of pearls that her mother had given her. She'd never worn them, except to Marcella's wedding.

Edgar dropped Marcella, decked out in a slim-waisted indigo dress, a gold lamé belt and gold shoes, at the front porch of Lucy's Cafe. He offered to walk her to the door, but she assured him she'd be fine on her own.

Polly Brown, Dora Mae Crawford, and Jewell Crabtree all dressed up a step or two beyond their Sunday best. The Pearle twins arrived in full regalia, including matching red pillbox hats. Some drove themselves, others hitched a ride with a husband or friend.

Linda Cruz parked her Honda in the spot that Stella had reserved for her near the door and entered to loud applause and the occasional whistles from Eva Jo. She was cute, as always, but with a little extra flare for the evening, courtesy of a black crepe skirt and white satin gauze top, a simple red bag, and red flats.

Twenty-one women, including a few who had not attended a Rosebud Circle meeting in years, chatted and laughed and ate around the three largest tables. Three or four women came up with the news that they had broken the all-time attendance record. The sound volume ebbed and expanded in a sporadic crescendo of sorts, depending upon whether they were laughing or catching their breath.

THERE WAS ONE TRAFFIC LIGHT IN MORGAN CROSSROADS. Lucy's Cafe sat just south of the intersection. To the north and across the street from Lucy's, a dozen pickup trucks and a car or two parked next to Brown's General Store. The porch was full of baggy overalls, bellies framed by stretched suspenders, and the occasional pair of khakis, all belonging to men whose other halves had gone to their secret shindig.

Across the porch rail, just below the busy rocking chairs, Ollie Smith flipped burgers and roasted ears of fresh sweet corn.

Henry slapped the screen door open and announced that any man who wanted a RC Cola and a bag of chips had better get inside and grab them.

"They've actually done it," Dave Crabtree said, staring past the traffic light toward the cafe. "Those women have pulled off a big to-do without telling a single man what they're doing in there."

"One of us ought to march over and walk right in just like he didn't know better," Grumpy said.

"Yep, and watch the look on their faces," Dave said.

"You mean the look they're gonna have when they watch

Eva Jo and Dora Mae team up and whack the poor guy upside the head with a couple of skillets," Henry said.

"I figured between them and another one or two, somebody in that bunch would spill the beans," Ollie said.

Henry patted Edgar on the shoulder. "Edgar here, he couldn't even use his lawyer voice to get anything out of Lorraine Haley."

"That's bad when we can't get her to talk. Normally you could go in there to get a steak cut or maybe pick up a pound of hamburger, and she'd blabber on about some off the wall thing. Most of the time, you'd have no clue what she was yappin' about," Grumpy said.

"There's no telling in this world what they'll come up with tonight," Ollie said. "There ain't been that many fancy hairdos in this place at one time since that country western singer, what was his name?"

"Porter Wagoner," overalls in the last chair hollered out.

"That's him. He did a show down at the old community center. You shoulda seen those ladies. There were beehives and bird nests and every other kind of hairdo there that night. The only other time was when Edgar and Marcella got married. There were enough fancy hairdos around that day to do for a lifetime," Ollie said. "Would you believe my wife had so much hair spray mixed up in her hair that her head was like a ball of cotton candy for about a week? I'm telling you it was. I slept on her pillow because she sure didn't need it."

Laughs, grunts, and knee slaps of agreement rolled from one end of the porch to the other.

"Ya'll come on down here and grab a burger or two. Watch that corn, though. It's so juicy you could squirt somebody in the eye when you bite into it," Ollie said. "And it'll burn you."

STELLA TAPPED HER SPOON ON THE EDGE OF HER EMPTY GLASS. Marcella patted her lips with a napkin and stepped to the podium that Morgan Chapel, the church across the street, lent for the occasion. "Ladies, most of us have been Rosebud Circle members for decades. And except for a few, like Lorraine Haley, we're old enough to remember the days when we all walked to our Tuesday morning meetings. Tonight, we have the privilege of welcoming Linda Cruz into our group."

Eva Jo nudged Linda toward the podium as Marcella invited her.

The Pearle twins began the clapping with a rapid but barely audible fingers against palm motion. By the time the wave of applause reached Dora Mae, it had crescendoed to a light roar. Eva Jo ripped the air with a whistle or two.

Linda Cruz held up a hand. "Thank you so much. You can stop now," she said, laughing and wishing away the warmth that had rushed across her face.

"See Honey, I told you they'd all be glad to have you," Marcella said as she moved to her seat.

"I just don't know what to say. Is this how it feels to win an Oscar?"

"If any of us ever win one, we'll let you know," Polly shouted.

"I didn't expect any of this. I thought we'd get together, eat a piece of cake, and talk about the men for a while."

Stella pointed a shaking finger toward the front window. "They're talking about us this time."

"We're about to wear them out," Polly said.

"Tell us a little about yourself," Marcella said.

Linda gave a light version of her background–high school

cheerleader, top of her class in her pharmacy program, the only niece to the childless uncle who had owned the local drugstore before her.

"How about men?" Lorraine Haley asked.

"What men?" Linda chuckled.

"There must be a few waiting in line," Lorraine said. "I mean, as pretty as you are. Good steady job."

"And well educated," Marcella added with an air of pride. "Fellows should like that about you."

"If I were a guy, I'd be banging on your door every morning," Eva Jo said.

"Well, I'm sorry I can't offer you anything juicier about my love life," Linda said. "But, you'll be the first to know if somebody shows up."

Eva Jo raised her tea glass in a toast. "Here's to Linda finding a man."

The other women joined in and with the sound of glasses clinking against each other, the first ever top secret Thursday evening meeting of the Rosebud Circle was over.

Some ladies chose to walk home. Edgar was waiting in the parking lot when Marcella stepped out. Eva Jo started her pickup truck and fumigated the parking lot. White smoke hung in the air for several minutes after she drove away.

———

"WHAT WAS ALL THAT NOISE ABOUT," HENRY ASKED FROM HIS recliner.

"What noise?" Polly said.

"All that clapping and whistling. We could hear you ladies all the way to the store."

"Nothing. Just having a little fun."

"What did you all talk about?"

"You should have had some of that cheesecake. It's all gone, but you would have liked it."

"So, are you going to tell me now what was so secret about whatever you women did?"

"Secret? We got together and ate like we always do." Polly said with a shrug.

Henry looked at Polly, scratched the side of his head, and left the room.

CHAPTER THREE

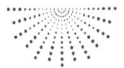

BED SHEETS AND PILLOW CASES FLAPPED IN THE WIND, absorbing the crisp spring air. Marcella had hung her laundry out for six decades and missed doing so after she married Edgar and moved with him into their new home.

Her laundry room had the latest appliances, space to hang whatever she needed, and built-in granite countertops where she could fold clothes and sew. But none of those niceties could make up for the fresh clean scent of laundry dried in breezy Whipper County, Alabama air. With her first load hung on the lines, she was ecstatic.

"Is that what you'd hope for?" Edgar asked.

"I could not ask for more perfect clothes lines," Marcella said, swooning.

With Henry Brown's help, Edgar had gathered his few carpentry and mechanical skills and had dug holes to install four posts beyond the patio garden behind the house. Between the posts, they had strung two sets of clothes lines. They stood on the patio, arms crossed, admiring their handiwork.

"How are the blisters?" Henry asked, pointing to Edgar's hands.

"Blisters," Marcella said as she thrust her hand out toward Edgar. "Let me see. Do you need a bandage?"

"I'll be fine," Edgar said as he showed her two blisters on one hand and a larger one on the other.

"Let me guess. You didn't dig too many post holes in Texas," Henry said.

"No, I don't suppose I did," Edgar said, grinning. "I owned a few hand tools, but except for tightening a door hinge or hanging a picture, I rarely used them."

"That's okay," Marcella said with her chin set. "He did other things that were just as demanding, and with the least bit of coaching, I believe he could do anything he needed to."

Edgar rubbed Marcella's shoulder with one hand and surveyed the blister on the other. "I'll be fine. They'll be gone in a couple days."

Henry excused himself, saying that he needed to get back to the store. Brown's General Store could do without him, but not for long.

———

EDGAR SHOWERED AND RETURNED TO THE PATIO, DRESSED IN A suit and tie, his silver hair groomed.

"My, you look handsome," Marcella said. "What time is your meeting?"

"An hour and fifteen minutes," Edgar said.

"You'd better get going."

He kissed Marcella with tenderness and retrieved his car keys from his pocket. "I'll be back this afternoon. It's a long meeting."

After selling his partnership in the law firm in Texas,

Edgar had arranged his life to allow as much leisure time as he wanted. He'd had plenty of time to travel and even more time to share his life with Jesse and Gloria, the niece and nephew he adopted when their mother died at a young age in an automobile accident. There were also the three grandsons that Gloria had provided him—small guys with endless stores of energy.

In Morgan Crossroads, life was different. There was little traffic noise, except when the occasional log truck rumbled and rattled through on its way to the mill in Porterville. The house was quiet without the grandchildren. They were still in Texas, but not for much longer, he hoped.

His and Marcella's wedding was several months in the past. They had traveled to Paris on their honeymoon and on a cruise that the townspeople had given them for a wedding gift.

Now that the wedding and the trips were over, Marcella's calendar was as full as ever. This despite her age being somewhere north of seventy. He was glad to see her enjoying every day of her life and wouldn't slow her down if he could. But while she zipped around Whipper County, if driving twenty-five miles per hour qualified as zipping, he twiddled around in search of something to pass the time.

He noticed that rarely a day went by without someone, usually one whom Marcella had taught in school, calling to ask her opinion about something. How long should I sear this roast before I put the lid on the pot? Or, does the salad fork go to the left or right of the plate? Grumpy had called her just the day before and asked what was causing black edges on his rose petals. If she didn't know the answer to a question, she'd always promise to find out what it was and call them back. And she never let them down.

Edgar had sometimes felt as though he were dragging

behind his wife. She was close to his age, yet he watched her move around as if her feet weighed nothing. Even on those days when arthritis showed itself, she kept it to herself. It was off to Lucy's Cafe for a Rose Bud Circle meeting, or out to Eva Jo's for one thing or another. When a family out in the cove needed help after the father had fallen ill, Marcella was the first one there with a box of food she'd gathered from her own pantry. What she didn't have on hand, she'd picked up at Haley's Grocery on the way. It was what her Papa would have done, she'd told him.

And there he found himself wishing for his own constructive thing to do. That's when a card asking for donations had come in the mail addressed to Marcella. "We would appreciate your donation of money or time," it said just above a photo of men and women leaving a food pantry with their hands full and their children tagging along behind them.

The Help Society in Huntsville provided housing, food, and other forms of assistance for displaced families. Edgar, never one to leave his attorney background behind, thoroughly vetted the organization. He found that it was one that he might like to become involved with.

Today, six months later, he was on his way to a Help Society budget meeting.

———

Marcella watched Edgar leave the driveway and returned to her laundry. Using a technique she'd learned as a young girl, she took a bedsheet from the line, folding it in just a few moves. She reached for another one, then stopped, frozen in place.

"Oh, my," she said to the breeze.

She left the remaining laundry on the line and dashed to the kitchen. Her eyes tightened to focus on the hand-writing that dotted the wall calendar next to the telephone. She gasped.

"I've forgotten his birthday." She held her palm to her forehead. "How could I have forgotten his birthday? I've not even baked a cake or bought a gift."

She found her baked goods cookbook and fumbled through it for a diabetic-friendly cake recipe. How in the world do I bake a cake for a diabetic? When a photo of a chocolate cake caught her attention, she made mental notes of the ingredients, then took a cursory inventory of her pantry shelves.

Marcella still preferred to use the heavy gray and blue stoneware bowl that had been her mother's. It was a gentle connection to the mother she never knew, the one who had lost her life while giving birth to her.

"Let's see." Marcella poured flour into the bowl, then whispered as she found each ingredient and measured it into the mix. "Cocoa. Sugar substitute. Oil."

She poured the batter into pans as fast as she dared and slid them into the pre-heated oven. She set the oven timer and temperature according to the instructions and left it while she finished gathering the laundry from the clothesline.

"EVA JO. HONEY, AM I GLAD YOU'RE HOME." SHE TOOK HALF A breath, just long enough for Eva Jo to respond.

"Are you all right? What's going on?"

"I'm fine now, but I may not be later this afternoon. Can you come over? Now?"

"What's wrong?" Eva Jo asked.

"Mud pie," Marcella said, surveying the collapsed cake.

"Mud pie? What about it?"

"That's what Edgar's birthday cake looks like. I need you to fix it before he comes home from his meeting."

"Slow down. You sound like you're about to breathe your last—"

"Honey," Marcella said. "You won't believe what I've done."

"You made a mud pie for Edgar's birthday?"

"I forgot his first birthday."

"He's older than you. You weren't around to remember it."

"No, no. His first as a married man, Eva Jo. I have forgotten the first birthday my husband would ever have with a wife."

"Ohhh. That might not be so good."

"How do you suppose I did that? Are you on your way, Honey? You've got to fix this cake for me."

Marcella had never been so glad to hear the squeaks, squawks, and rattles that announced the arrival of Eva Jo's old pickup truck and its owner.

Before Eva Jo could shove open her door, Marcella was off the porch and half-way to the truck. "I thought you'd never get here," Marcella said.

"Honey, it's barely been five minutes since you called. I had to change my shoes. You wouldn't have liked it if I wore my milking boots in your kitchen," Eva said. "Let me see this disaster that has you all flustered."

In the kitchen, Eva Jo stood with a hand propped on each

hip and stared first at the cake, then at Marcella. The cake. Marcella.

"Well?" Marcella said.

"Well, what?"

"Can you fix it?"

"I'm not so sure about that. I'm not in the miracle business. You know that, don't you?"

"You made our wedding cake. That's good enough for me," Marcella said.

"Whatever disease this thing has, it's terminal," Eva Jo said, sliding the mystery cake into the garbage can. "Grab me an apron and a mixing bowl."

Eva Jo asked what was in the cake. Marcella showed her the recipe and the ingredients she had used.

Eva Jo glanced down the list of ingredients and closed the book. She handed it to Marcella. "Let's bake a cake."

"Now, remember, Edgar is a diabetic," Marcella said.

"Got it. Slide that bag of flour over here."

"It's beautiful," Marcella said as she hugged Eva Jo. "Maybe I should stick to cooking pot roast or shepherd's pie."

"That might not be a bad plan," Eva Jo said through a grin.

"This cake is quite a work of art, considering the short time you took to bake it," Marcella said.

The layers had come out of the oven a beautiful light golden brown with just the right height and sugar-free. After a quick search through her memory, Eva Jo had made a thick creamy frosting she'd used for a diabetic nephew's graduation cake. Displayed on an earthenware pedestal stand, the cake looked like a blue ribbon prize winner.

"I simply cannot believe that I forgot Edgar's birthday," Marcella said, shaking her head.

"I wouldn't get too shook up about it," Eva Jo said. "I've had three husbands and I can't remember any of their birthdays." She laughed, jiggling like a bowl of gelatin.

Marcella's forehead furrowed. "Yes, but you didn't even like the last two. I love Edgar and I've daydreamed for over forty years of baking a birthday cake for him. I would have the house cleaned and in order. I'd hear his car stop in the driveway and run to the door in my apron to welcome him home after a long day at the office."

"Honey, don't you think that sounds more like a *Leave It to Beaver* rerun than real life?" Eva Jo said.

"Well, I'm sure it does to some women, with so many having their own careers. And that's okay," she said, pointing a finger at no one. "I had my career as an educator. And I'm thrilled women are coming on in more advanced fields. Take Doctor Crofton and Linda Cruz at the pharmacy for examples, and those who are attorneys and politicians. But greeting him with my apron on and something good to eat in the kitchen is still what I dreamed about for all those years. It's what I had hoped to do today."

Eva Jo pointed toward the garage. "You'd better get with it, then. He's home. Grab your apron."

As Marcella opened the door that led to the garage, Eva Jo slipped out the front door, eased it shut behind her, then rattled and roared her way down the driveway.

THE ROSES WERE METICULOUSLY ARRANGED, A VARIETY OF twelve different tea roses.

"Look at these," Marcella said, smelling one, then another. "They're beautiful. What's the occasion, Dear?"

"The occasion is that I have the privilege of coming home to the most beautiful woman this planet has ever seen," Edgar said. He bent and kissed her forehead. "What is that delightful something I smell?"

She took the roses from him. "Follow me. I have the perfect spot for these."

In the center of the breakfast table sat the monument that two hours earlier had been a hastily concocted bowl of flour, eggs, and other ingredients scattered across the kitchen counter.

"I didn't know you baked, too," Edgar said. "Did you bake this?"

"In a way," she said, a blush settling into her cheeks.

"Great," he said, looking around for forks and plates. "Who gets the honor of slicing?"

"I do," Marcella said, grinning. "I've waited decades for this opportunity."

She sliced the cake, insuring that each piece was the same size. Then, smiling, slid the first slice onto a plate for Edgar.

"Happy birthday, Dear." She kissed his cheek, then used a napkin to wipe the lipstick from his cheek. "Sorry. I doubt you'd want to wear that anywhere else."

"It's delicious," he said with cake in his mouth. "Should I keep my glucometer handy?"

"I hope not."

CHAPTER FOUR

THE ATMOSPHERE AT POLLY'S HOUSE OF BEAUTY WAS BACK TO normal. Dora Mae Crawford stopped by to chat, but still had a few good days of wear left in the hairdo she'd worn to the dinner.

Polly took a clean apron from the storage closet and wrapped it around Jewell Crabtree. "Where'd all this wet straw come from?"

"Don't ask me," Jewell said. "It happened when I went out to feed Him and Her. You know, those horses we inherited last week when our neighbor moved."

Dora Mae had a staccato way of speaking, with a kind of inaudible smacking that accentuated drawn-out words. "We need to find Linda Cruz a man," she said, somehow turning man into two syllables.

"We need to do what?" Polly said in an elevated pitch.

"She said we need to find a guy for Linda," Jewell said.

"I know what she said," Polly said, accidentally tugging a little hard on Jewell's hair. "Sorry, Honey."

"There's got to be somebody around here that would make a good husband," Dora Mae said.

"When did we become a matchmaking service?" Polly said.

"Linda is one of us, you know," Jewell said.

"She is, and that's exactly why we need to stay out of her business. Which one of us even knows a single man who could interest a bright young lady like her?" Polly said.

Dora Mae got up and poured herself a cup of coffee. "There's that little guy who lives behind the Dairy Bar–what's his name? Jerry or Jimmy, something like that."

"Mason," Jewell said. "Not a suitable candidate."

"What's wrong with him?" Dora Mae asked.

"Nothing except that he's been married for at least five years," Polly said.

"When did that happen?" Dora Mae said.

"When he lived in Huntsville. His wife lives the other side of Porterville. He lives in Morgan Crossroads," Jewell said. "Never have lived together, as far as I know."

"What kind of marriage is that?" Dora Mae asked.

"The kind that keeps him off the available for marriage list," Polly said.

"Well, I'm going to keep my eyes open. The social column in the *Gazette* has been a little scant lately. Anyway, we need another wedding around here," Dora Mae said. "Keep some excitement going, you know."

"Let me guess. You've got some good-looking young man up your sleeve that you think would be Linda's Prince Charming," Polly said.

"Well, there's that Jenkins boy that lives out past the cemetery. He works on air conditioners and refrigerators and such," Dora Mae said.

"What makes you think he's shopping for a lady?" Jewell said.

"We can't just force a guy to like somebody, you know," Polly said.

"Well, I know that," Dora Mae said. "But that young man is just far too nice for someone like Linda to miss out on. Linda's nice. He's nice. Maybe they could get together and someday they'd have a boatload of nice kids."

"So you think Linda needs her air conditioner worked on." Jewell said.

"No, but she mentioned that the little refrigerator she keeps her lunch in wasn't keeping her water bottles cold enough."

"I know who would be the perfect match for Linda," Jewell said.

"Don't tell me he's that guy that pumps out septic tanks," Dora Mae said.

"Where did that come from?" Jewell asked.

"I don't know. Maybe because he's the last choice around here."

"Well, he's always been a complete gentleman when we've called him," Polly said. "Last time, he figured out there was something wrong with it and dug up the whole thing. We haven't had to call him back since."

"Oh, that's fine and good, not that your septic tank has anything to do with Linda Cruz. I know the man's a real friendly fellow. But he's already been married four times," Dora Mae said.

"How would you know that?" Jewell asked.

Dora Mae hitched her right eyebrow as high as it would go, as if to say it was her gift to the world to know everybody's business.

"Eva Jo Clomper's been married three or four times, and she's fairly normal," Polly said.

"Yes, but she's too old to marry Linda," Dora Mae said.

She looked around the room, wondering why even the eyes peering from under the noisy hair dryers were staring at her.

"I think Jeremiah Downs would make a perfect husband to Linda Cruz," Jewell said.

"Who said she wanted to marry a minister?" Gertrude Gleaves yelled out from under the hair dryer.

"What's wrong with that?" Jewell yelled back.

"Nothing's wrong with being a minister, but he's just here temporarily. He could be gone to Chattanooga or somewhere else this time next month."

"Gertrude, the poor guy's been putting up with us at Morgan Chapel for two or three years. I don't think he's going to just up and move away," Polly said.

"We need to get the two of them together some way," Jewell said.

"Doesn't she go to the Methodist church in Porterville?" Polly asked.

Gertrude pointed toward the south. "I thought she went to that little Pentecostal church down at–"

"Her uncle was a Lutheran or something like that," Dora Mae said.

"Well, I'm sure she'd be flexible if the right man came along," Jewell said.

"DO YOU KNOW WHAT I THINK?" BEFORE MARCELLA COULD reply, Eva Jo continued. "I think we need to find that girl a man."

Marcella lowered her coffee cup to the table. "What are you up to?"

Eva Jo slid a dessert plate in front of Marcella. "How

about a chunk of pineapple upside cake to go with that?" She sliced a corner piece for each of them.

"Sure, why not? Find what girl a man?" Marcella said.

"Linda Cruz. She says she's in the market for a man and we need to help her out, don't you think?"

"I think that's a personal matter. How would you like it if people snooped around trying to find you a man?"

"At this age? I'd think they were crazy. But if I was her age, I'd be wishing for all the help I could find," Eva Jo said. "Maybe I'd have come across one that would hang around for a while."

"I don't know," Marcella said. "That just seems like we'd be stepping into her personal life. She might not appreciate that."

"Well, for starters, I've got a grandson that could use a little help in that department."

"Which one?"

"Michael. He's a good boy with a good heart and it's time he found himself somebody to marry."

"Eva Jo, Linda might not want our help. Did you ever think of that?"

"Yes, but not for long. She as much as said there were no men in her life."

Marcella took another bite of cake. "Umm. Honey, you have outdone yourself with this one. I love it."

"Good. I'm glad you're not worried about calories," Eva Jo said.

"I'll have to think your idea over. Most of the single men I know are single because they're widowers. They're as old as we are," Marcella said. "She wouldn't want a man that old."

"I'll see if I can persuade Michael to get up and go after her. He'll sure never find a better girl. That's for sure."

WITH THE LOW HUMIDITY, THE GENTLE BREEZE, AND A BRIGHT blue sky painted with thin strokes of white, it was a beautiful day to live in Morgan Crossroads, Alabama. Marcella and Edgar walked from their house, past the drugstore and Brown's General Store. At the light—the only traffic signal in town—they crossed Highway Fourteen and slowed from a walk to a stroll.

Marcella had always loved this section of Main Street. Except for the years she attended The University of Texas, she had lived just a block off Main. That was, until she married Edgar at a few years past seventy.

Bricks covered Main in a herringbone pattern of red from the light south to the block past Haley's Grocery. A black iron fence topped with gothic style finials surrounded Morgan Chapel, and from there south toward the Dairy Bar, almost every home owner along those blocks had a fence of either pickets or ornamental metal. Flower beds lined the brick portion of Main Street between the fences and the sidewalk. Sycamores, sugar maples, and gingkoes provided shade for people who stopped to chat.

"Do you think Jesse would ever move here?" Marcella asked.

"He seems to enjoy his visits, but I suspect it has more to do with his incredibly nice mom than with the geographic location," Edgar said. "Why?"

"You make me blush. Stop that." She play-swatted his arm.

"It's true," Edgar said. "Do you want him to move here?"

"I would love to have him and Gloria both here. And the grandchildren. But you know Jesse's alone and . . ."

"You thought perhaps you could come up with a wife for him."

"Why did you say that?"

"Is it true?" Edgar said with one eyebrow cocked.

"I don't know that I could come up with a wife for him, but don't you think his company would be nice?"

"Yes, it would, but I'm not so sure that he would want to leave his job behind. You know Jesse's tenured at the university, don't you?"

"I had forgotten that, but yes, I do."

"How easy do you think it would be for a literature professor to find a job in this area?" Edgar said.

"Well, there's The University of Alabama in Huntsville. Have you heard there are plans for a new high school in Porterville?" Marcella said.

"He may not be interested in leaving post-secondary education."

In the block where the brick pavement ended, they found a weathered wrought-iron bench and sat for a rest in the shade of a sycamore. There were several such benches scattered along both sides of Main Street, most shaded from morning to evening. But this bench, while quite public, was their little secret place. She laid her head on Edgar's shoulder. Closing her eyes for a moment, she took in the sounds of chirping birds filling the trees with joyous life.

In a large decorative garden just beyond their bench, a path of natural flagstones curved its way between irises, tulips, and violets. "Aren't they beautiful?" Marcella asked.

"I like the tulips," Edgar said. "Especially the yellow varieties."

White, purple, and yellow had never looked so refreshing. Around the edges, red bricks stood on end, forming a border, shoulder to shoulder like little soldiers. Across the street the lot was full of trees, every shade of green.

"What if there is a wife here for Jesse?" Marcella asked.

"Dear, are you thinking of going into the matchmaking business?"

"Whatever makes you ask that?" Marcella twitched, wiping her hands lightly along her skirt as if it could use ironing.

CHAPTER FIVE

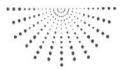

THE RIDE DOWN KRENSHAW'S HILL MIGHT HAVE BEEN EASIER had Michael Clomper not taken it head first. On his back. At night. And the landing might have been softer had his mountain bike not followed him and landed on top of him.

Michael had been home less than a week from a National Guard deployment to the Middle East. Before he left, he had ridden his bike every day if time allowed. From the time he received his first mountain bike on his tenth birthday, Michael had been serious about cross-country biking. He rode through hollows and across hills on logging roads and trails across Whipper County, training for local or regional competitions. He looked forward to the day that he might compete on a national level.

The deployment had sidetracked his competitive ambitions for a while, and he had looked forward to riding again. He had worked on his bike for most of the day, cleaning it and servicing it after months of being stowed away in a storage room in his grandmother's barn.

Dough Springs Road was a ribbon of narrow and winding asphalt that rose from the valley floor just north of

Morgan Crossroads, up to the ridge that ran along the west side of the valley toward Porterville. It was the road that the locals used to mark the western boundary of Whipper County. He had intended to ride Dough Springs Road up the ridge, then cut off on Dodson trail and follow it back down to where it circled into Morgan Crossroads near Lorraine Haley's grocery store.

By the time Michael reached the ridge where he had hoped to cut off on Dodson trail, the sun was well on its way out of sight. He miscalculated his speed in a curve and lost control of his bike right at the top of a mostly gravel hill that sloped not so gently downward to the pasture directly behind Denton Krenshaw's dairy barn.

"What the . . ." Denton rushed out of the barn to see where the rumbling and crashing sound was coming from. He was just in time to see the bike land, with Michael in his yellow touring shirt under it, next to a pine tree a few yards up the hillside. "Oh, God."

Denton scrambled up the hill, losing his own footing once. "Are you okay, son?" Denton said, addressing Michael the way he did any male below thirty years of age.

Michael groaned, and through dirty eyelids, tried to gather his bearings. "I think so."

Denton made sure Michael had no broken bones, then lifted the bike off of him. Once he was sure there were no life-threatening wounds, he helped Michael to his feet and together they hobbled and limped to the house. He helped Michael clean and bandage the dozen scrapes and cuts that covered his arms and legs.

"How is it you wound up sliding downhill into my yard?" Denton asked.

"I was up on Dough Springs Road riding, getting a little practice in."

"After dark? Practicing?" Denton scratched his head. "Wouldn't it be better to do that in the daytime?"

"There was plenty of light when I left home," Michael said. "Time got away from me, that's all."

"Looks like that wasn't all that got away from you."

"Can I borrow your telephone?" Michael asked. He had left his cell phone at home, thinking there would be no coverage on the ridge.

"Sure, but you might have to scoot your chair a bit."

Denton took the receiver from the wall phone and gave it to Michael. "Who do you want to call?"

"My grandmother, Eva Jo Clomper."

Denton's face lit. "You're that Clomper boy that just came back from over in the Middle East, aren't you?"

"Yes, sir."

"Well, I'll be. I thought you looked familiar, but sometimes familiar doesn't mean much when you meet in strange situations. What's her number?"

Michael recited his grandmother's phone number, and listened while Denton carried on a ten-minute conversation, covering everything from the weather to how he had heard Michael crash-landing behind his barn.

"She'll be out in a while. Your grandmother's a good woman. You know that, don't you?"

"Yes, sir."

"We've known each other since we were five or six years old. She was a rounder, Eva Jo was." Denton held a bag in front of Michael. "Cookie?"

"I saw her whip more than one boy when he'd try to steal a sandwich out of her lunch sack. You won't ever hear him admit it, but she wore Henry Brown completely out one day in the third grade because he wouldn't quit messing with her hair."

Michael grinned. "She did? Are you serious?"

"I'm as serious as I know how to be." Denton laughed. "Ol' Henry moved his desk all the way over to the other side of the room. I bet it was six months before he'd even speak to her after that."

"She's never told me that story," Michael said.

"I'm pretty sure there are a bunch of stories like that that she ain't told you. Did she ever tell you about the time she hit Grumpy's daddy over the head with a milk bucket?"

"Granny did that?"

"Just ask her about it sometime. Better wait until you catch her in a good mood, though."

THE NEXT MORNING, EVA JO HELPED MICHAEL INTO THE truck and drove him to Porterville for a medical checkup.

"You are one lucky young man," Doctor Crofton said. Sue Crofton was an attractive African-American lady and the only female doctor in the county. She maintained a practice in Huntsville and saw patients two days a week at an office she shared between Porterville and Morgan Crossroads.

"Nothing's broken, and you should be over the scrapes and bruises in a few days." She gave him a note on which she had written the name of an over-the-counter ointment for the scrapes and a prescription for a pain reliever to help with the aches. "Linda Cruz can help you with these at the pharmacy."

"Thanks," Michael said. He hobbled out to the parking lot and climbed into his grandmother's rusty old pickup truck.

"What exactly were you doing up by Krenshaw's hill at night, anyway?" Eva Jo asked with one eyebrow cocked. "I've been trying to figure that out and I just haven't come up with anything that makes sense."

"The same thing I told you last night, just taking a little joy ride. Feeling the wind in my face. A little exercise to keep my blood flowing."

"You know what I think? I think you went up there to meet somebody. Who was that girl you were sweet on before you were deployed? Amy somebody?"

"Granny! I went for a ride and lost track of time. That's all. And besides, Amy's at Penn State now."

"Well, then, my next question—"

"Granny, can we drop it?"

"Why didn't you turn around and come on back when you saw it was heading toward sundown? You know your daddy did almost the same thing when he was about your age. Broke everything he had except that hard head of his."

"He was on a motorcycle," Michael said, insinuating that the mode of transportation made a difference. "I went to see about a job. I thought there might still be somebody at the sawmill I could talk to. Maybe haul lumber or something."

"That place shut down two months ago. Old man Ferguson finally retired when he hit ninety, or eighty-nine, whatever it was," Eva Jo said.

"Granny, what about temporary work? You know, I can do carpentry and yard work. And I'm good at working on cars."

"I hear Linda Cruz is planning some remodeling at the drugstore. Maybe you can talk to her about it in a few minutes when you pick up your prescription."

CHAPTER SIX

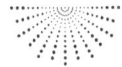

"I don't think that's going—" One end of the blue and white striped awning crashed to the sidewalk. "to fit," Linda Cruz said.

"Guess not," her uncle said.

"Maybe you should have stuck with filling prescriptions," she said, trying not to laugh.

Robert Benson, Linda Cruz's uncle, had owned Crossroads Pharmacy in Morgan Crossroads, Alabama for forty years when he retired and let Linda take over. "It looks like you'll have to find somebody else to hang that awning for you. Seems I might have misjudged my talents."

"Uncle Robert, I'm not exactly saying that I told you so, but apparently awnings aren't hung exactly the same way as picture frames," Linda said. "How about a cup of coffee?"

"I'll take you up on that offer."

Linda and her uncle left the awning hanging askew and walked to the rear of the drugstore. She poured a cup of coffee and added five sugar cubes and two extended splashes of creamer at his request. "How do you drink this stuff?" Linda asked.

Robert shot a look at her cup and said, "I should ask you the same question."

"What? This is my version of an iced mocha," she said with her nose slightly elevated. "An exquisitely prepared drink, if I say so myself."

"If God had intended coffee to be drunk cold, he would have caused it to grow in Antarctica. That's what I say."

The bell over the front door jangled when Eva Jo Clomper came in. She walked like a woman on a mission to the back counter where she zeroed in on Linda's uncle. "Robert, what's that sour look on your face about?"

"What look?" he said.

"You look like somebody squirted you in the face with lemon juice," Eva Jo said.

"He's okay," Linda said. "He just has no appreciation for modern coffee recipes."

Eva Jo said, "If my memory serves me right, he has no right to say anything about your coffee. Have you seen his? A little squirt of coffee in half a cup of cream and sugar." She looked over the display shelves. "I need some bandages. No need to show me. Just point."

Linda walked around the counter and led Eva Jo to the first aid section. "This box has an assortment of small bandages," she said, handing it to Eva Jo.

"Honey, I'll need something a lot bigger than those," Eva Jo said. "You got any about this big?" she asked, holding her hands to form a circle the size of a softball.

"What are you trying to bandage?" Linda asked.

"Michael. He lost control of his bicycle last night and beat himself up pretty good. I don't suppose you'd have anything big enough to bandage his pride, do you?"

Linda chuckled. "I don't think I can help you with that. I hope he'll be okay. Is he with you?"

"I tried to get him to come in, but he stayed out in the truck, nursing about a dozen bruises. He'll get over it if he'll just do what Doctor Crofton told him to do. She said he should be back to normal in three or four weeks, but to keep the worst cuts and scrapes covered for a few days."

Eva Jo laid Michael's prescription order on the counter and waited for Linda to fill it. She paid for her items and returned to her truck, hesitating for a minute to survey the upended awning that Linda and her uncle had left on the sidewalk.

"You hungry?" Eva Jo shifted the old pickup truck into a higher gear.

"What did you say?" Michael pointed to the rusty hole in the floorboard through which road and exhaust noise roared.

"Are you hungry?" she said with her volume cranked up a notch or two. She steered the old truck into the parking lot at Lucy's Cafe.

"That's not Marcella Peabody's new car, is it?" Michael asked as Eva Jo pulled in to a parking space next to the ivory-colored BMW.

"Yes, it is, sorta. And it's Garrison now. Marcella Garrison. Remember, she got married while you were gone. That's Edgar's car."

"I remember, but all my life she's been a Peabody. That's a hard name to forget."

"Well, try. She's proud to be a Garrison now."

"Has she still got that old Chevy, that antique one?" Michael asked.

"She sure does, and she'll drive that thing until the paint falls off it. I'm surprised Edgar talked her into riding in his car today."

Inside Lucy's Cafe, heavy plates and flatware clanged and

rattled as Stella cleared dishes from Edgar and Marcella's table.

Eva Jo stopped beside Marcella and asked, "Where's mine?"

Edgar stood and shook Michael's hand, introducing himself. "Will you join us? We were just about to order dessert, but we can wait." He started around to help Eva Jo with her chair, but she had seated herself before he was half-way there.

"Michael, what happened to you?" Marcella asked. "One of your grandmother's cows didn't get the best of you, did it?"

"No ma'am. My mountain bike did." Michael told her the story of how he had landed at the bottom of Krenshaw's hill.

"Dough Springs Road? That's a dangerous place at night," Marcella said.

Eva Jo chimed in. "I think he might have heard that from somebody else, too," she said with a wry grin aimed directly at Michael.

Edgar sensed that Michael might come out with the short end of the stick in this discussion. "What kind of work do you do?"

"I haven't found a permanent job since my discharge, but I've been looking." Michael took a long drink of iced tea. "I'm good with my hands—carpentry, painting, lawn care—things like that."

Marcella said, "Edgar, he could help you with those things you want done."

"Didn't Linda Cruz say she was remodeling the drugstore?" Eva Jo asked.

Michael visually followed the conversation from Marcella to Edgar, back to Marcella, then to his grandmother.

"From the looks of that awning earlier today, I'd say she

needs somebody's help," Eva Jo said, chuckling. "Poor thing was just hanging by one end, and the other end dragging the sidewalk."

Marcella shot Eva Jo a look that could not have been misinterpreted. *You're trying to get Michael and Linda together.*

Marcella tapped Edgar's arm. "Edgar, didn't you say you wanted some shelves and a workbench built in the garage?"

"I need those and I'd like to have a new fence behind the fireplace on the patio."

"There you go, Michael," Marcella said. "That would keep you busy for several days. And I'm sure Edgar would pay you well."

Michael's eyes brightened. "I could probably—"

"Have you seen Linda's awning?" Eva Jo said. "She'll need that fixed right quick, I'd say."

"I could ask her about doing that after I help Edgar," Michael said.

"What if that thing falls on somebody's head? They'd be as loony as a bat when they woke up," Eva Jo said.

Edgar watched Michael turn from his grandmother to Marcella, then back and forth, with an occasional stop in Edgar's area as if wondering if he might have a clue what was going on. "From the looks of those bandages I'd say it will be a few days before he tackles either job. You can start on mine whenever you want to, Michael. Let me know if you need money for supplies or tools," Edgar said.

"I'll do yours first, then I'll talk to Linda about her awning," Michael said.

"If she doesn't come up with somebody else to do it before then," Eva Jo said.

CHAPTER SEVEN

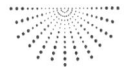

THE PORCH THAT SPANNED THE WIDTH OF BROWN'S GENERAL Store was a breeding ground for monumental tales. If one believed everything ever said on that porch, he might come away convinced that a commercial airliner had landed on the two-lane county road south of town. In reality, a crop-dusting plane had run out of gas and landed in Ollie Smith's pasture. There were tales of deer the size of horses and of the real Elvis stopping in for directions, thirty years after he had left the building for good.

"I'm telling you, I saw it with my own eyes," Dave Crabtree said. He held his hands ten inches apart. "That frog was this long if he was an inch."

The talking and tobacco spitting stopped when Ollie Smith pointed toward the intersection. "Would you look at that?"

Henry Brown left his rocking chair and leaned on the wooden porch rail. "Now that right there takes the cake."

"Isn't that Gertrude Gleaves's car?" Abe Jones asked.

"I believe so, but that ain't her driving it," Ollie said.

"That's Grumpy," Henry said.

A perfectly normal looking Oldsmobile had just turned at the light and headed south on Main Street, rumbling its way toward somewhere—in reverse. Grumpy was in line with other drivers who were traveling forward, but he was driving backward as if that were the accepted way to drive.

"Oooouch," Abe said. "Did you see what he did to my marigolds?"

"He'd better get that thing off the street before he wipes out somebody's fence," Ollie said.

"Why is he driving backward?" Henry asked.

"Maybe it won't go forward," Ollie said with a shrug. "Looks like he's headed toward his shop."

"I thought that was why he bought that old tow truck," Henry said.

"I'll see you fellows," Abe said. "There's a flower bed that needs a little loving."

Abe jumped in his tired old truck, its bed full of wheelbarrows, rakes, and shovels and drove off toward the wounded flower bed. He referred to every flower bed along Main Street as his and tended them as if they were his pride and joy.

He had been the full-time unofficial town gardener in Morgan Crossroads since he retired from his hotel maintenance job in Huntsville. Even before his retirement, he had lent his artistic touch to the community lawns and gardens, including those along the bricks of Main Street. Marcella and others swore that their vegetable gardens produced more when Abe tended them. He never charged for his services, but managed to live on the tips and gifts that people had given him over the years.

"WHY DON'T YOU INVITE JESSE, GLORIA, AND THE BOYS TO come for a few days?" Marcella asked.

Edgar closed his Dan Brown novel. "Are you sure you can handle so many of us at one time? Remember, you have that craft show in Porterville that you and Polly talked about."

"I'd be delighted to have them. You could take the boys to the Space Center in Huntsville, and Gloria might enjoy meeting some women around here. Maybe I could talk her into baking some of her delicious pastries. I don't know how she does it, but she can work miracles with a few apples and a bag of flour. By the way, I forgot to tell you the craft show won't be happening after all."

"Just thinking about her apple dumplings sends my blood sugar reeling," Edgar said.

"Maybe the four of you could go golfing or swimming."

"That would be great, but I'm not sure they can get away right now. Didn't Jesse say that he was going somewhere before his fall schedule starts?"

"Does he still have Spotlight?" Marcella asked. "That dog was the first thing I saw when Jesse stopped by to bring you back into my life."

"Spotlight is living like a king from what I've gathered. Jesse gave him his own room, complete with a queen-size bed."

Marcella gave a squinted look out of the corner of her eye.

"He did. I'm serious," Edgar said.

"Don't tell me that Spotlight has his own shower, too," Marcella said.

"I'll have to ask about that," Edgar said, rising from his recliner. "Can I get you a glass of iced tea?"

Just after eight o'clock the next morning, Marcella scurried to answer the front doorbell.

"Would you like to buy a raffle ticket, Mrs. Peabody?"

Before she could form a reply, the youngster on the porch continued. "You could win a week of dinners for two at Lucy's Cafe and six car washes at the Shell station in Porterville."

"I don't–"

"There's something else, too. A television or something like that."

"Who is it–"

"I sure would like to win. If I do, I get some prizes and my junior league football team gets some new uniforms."

"How much–"

"I sure hope they ain't that ugly green like they were last year," the little guy said.

"Aren't that ugly green," Marcella snapped out in her former school teacher voice. "Joshua, does your father know you're out knocking on doors so early?"

"You know my dad?" the boy asked with a wadded up forehead and squinted eyes.

"Yes, Joshua, I taught Johnny Mack Durant for several years. Does he know you're out knocking on doors this early, or do we need to call him?"

"You don't have to do that. He's sitting right down the road waiting for me to finish up so we can go fishing. You want to buy a raffle ticket? They're just five dollars a piece."

Marcella fished a ten-dollar bill from her purse and checked the time on the grandfather clock across the room. She took two tickets from the boy and suggested he go fishing before he finished his door knocking. "And my name is Mrs. Garrison now."

THE DAY BEGAN SOMEWHERE SOUTH OF BAD AND DESCENDED into a state of absolutely awful. Eva Jo phoned to say that her washing machine had decided to take a few days off. She asked Marcella if she could borrow her washer and dryer for a couple hours. She said she couldn't stand hanging around a laundromat that long. "It wouldn't be so bad if they'd get some fresh magazines in there. How many times can you read the same story about some actor going through his umpteenth divorce before you want to pull your hair out, anyway?"

"Of course you may," Marcella said. "You'll have to excuse the mess, though."

"What mess? I'd have to crawl around on my knees to find a speck of dust in your house."

"It's worse than that. Edgar got up this morning and walked to the kitchen to make his pot of coffee and stepped right onto a floor covered with water."

"Don't tell me the laundry room is out of commission," Eva Jo said. "How many mops do you need me to bring?"

"We got the water up, so there'll be no need for mops. The leak is behind the refrigerator. It's the water supply for the ice maker, Edgar thinks. He cut off the valve to it and the leak stopped. I suppose the refrigerator will be in the middle of the kitchen floor and the plumbers will have to cut the water off while they repair the leak."

"How am I going to do laundry with no water?"

"Is Michael working anywhere today?" Marcella asked.

"He was going over to help Linda Cruz with her awning."

"Can you call him and ask if he'll put Linda off for a while? He might be able to repair our leak."

Eva Jo held the phone to her side for a moment. *And*

Michael misses another day presenting himself to the most eligible woman in town.

"If we don't fix the leak, you don't do laundry and we may not eat lunch," Marcella said.

"I'll see if I can find him," Eva Jo said, staring at Michael's cell phone on the counter.

Two hours later, Eva Jo's rattling pickup truck announced Michael's and her arrival.

Marcella met them at the door. "What is that dragging under your truck?"

"It's just the muffler," Eva Jo said. "Nothing important."

"Well, I'd say it's important. I don't believe it would be there if it weren't important."

"That's her early warning system," Michael said with a smile. "There's no risk of her sneaking up on anyone."

"I'd never noticed that you wore a mustache," Marcella said, pointing to the fresh growth above his lip. "You aren't trying to impress a particular young lady, are you?"

Eva Jo elbowed Michael and said to Marcella, "Show him where the leak is so I can get this laundry done."

Marcella led Michael to the kitchen. "It ran from beneath the refrigerator over there." She pointed out an area that covered most of the kitchen.

Michael surveyed the situation and devised a way to nudge the massive commercial-size refrigerator from its place.

"Watch out," Eva Jo said just as the fitting broke away from the pipe in the wall.

By the time Eva Jo and Marcella found the valve to shut off the main water supply, a mess that was earlier restricted to wet stone on the kitchen floor had turned into a much larger catastrophe that included soaked carpet in the den and two hallways.

Marcella stared at the carpet. Eva Jo stared with her. Michael, with arms crossed and a puzzled look on his face, stared at the broken pipe. No one spoke for at least sixty seconds.

"I didn't see Edgar's car," Eva Jo said. "Is it in the garage?"

"He's gone to the hardware store in Porterville," Marcella said.

"What's he doing there?"

"To shop for a pipe wrench, I believe he said."

"Would he know how to use it?"

"Of course he would," Marcella said with a quick turn of her head toward Eva Jo.

"Has he ever used one?"

"Perhaps. But even if he hasn't, I know he'd be a quick study. He'd pick it up right away."

Michael forced back a snicker.

Eva Jo tried, but couldn't hold it any longer. "I love Edgar like a brother, Honey. And I'm awfully proud you found him and married him. But owning a pipe wrench doesn't make him a plumber any more than frying chicken makes me Julia Child."

By mid-afternoon, Michael and Edgar had torn out half of the drywall material behind the refrigerator. It wasn't exactly a show of award-winning workmanship, but they could now see more of the problem area than they knew what to do with.

Edgar had shown much less emotion over the current plumbing issue than anyone else. Marcella paced the floor like a nervous cat. Eva Jo asked one too many times how long it would take to get the laundry working. After hearing, "I

55

have no idea," enough times, the women climbed into Marcella's old Chevy and headed to Lucy's Cafe for lunch.

"I think that's probably enough," Edgar said. "Any more and we'll have to explain ourselves to two women."

"What are you going to tell them?" Michael asked.

"We could tell them we wanted to be certain that the real plumbers would have enough room to work."

"Have you called a plumber?"

"No, I haven't. What type of plumbing is that, in case they ask?"

"Just tell them you can see copper piping through the hole in the wall and you believe a valve has broken off," Michael said.

Edgar scanned the list of important numbers that Marcella kept on a note board near the phone and found a plumber in Porterville.

"Someone will be here within the hour," Edgar said. "I'll call Lucy's and let Marcella and Eva Jo know."

"I'm glad you suggested they eat lunch out. Granny would have worn me out by now. 'You fellas done?' she'd say. 'How much more do you like? Can I do my laundry yet?'"

"I never made that suggestion, but I agree with you anyway." Edgar motioned for Michael to follow him to the garage where they each picked up an electric fan.

"These should help dry the flooring," Edgar said.

"Don't you think you'd better hire somebody to clean this up? I think I'm in just a little over my head," Michael said.

"You're right. But don't feel bad. When I lived in Texas, I just called a plumber or electrician or whoever I needed when something broke. I suppose I'm just trying to look as though I'm taking care of it. That's what men around here do. They see something broken and they fall head first into repairing it. But Marcella will probably feel better about it if I've already called the professionals when she comes back."

A few minutes well spent on the Internet resulted in an appointment for a crew from Huntsville to arrive first thing the next day.

Edgar handed Michael two twenty-dollar bills. "How about running over to Lucy's for some lunch? I'd like a salad and whatever soup she has today. Take my car," he said, holding the keys.

"Oh, no. If I did to that BMW what I did to that wall, you'd kill me. I'll just walk. It's not far."

"Take it anyway," Edgar said, again offering the key to Michael. "It's just a car. There are others where that one came from."

The plumbers came as scheduled and repaired the pipes in less time than anyone expected.

Eva Jo did three loads of laundry and went home.

Edgar showered while Marcella made sandwiches for dinner. "The less time I have to stare at that hole, the better."

As PROMISED, THE DOORBELL RANG PROMPTLY AT SEVEN THE next morning. Marcella opened the door to find two men in carpenters' overalls and smiles. They introduced themselves as being from the home repair company. One was tall and stout and wore an Auburn University cap. The other was shorter and wiry, wearing a University of Alabama cap. She showed them into the kitchen where Edgar was studying the repaired valve.

After a few minutes of surveying the damage, the tallest of the men wrote an estimate and showed it to Edgar, who accepted it with little more than a glance at the cost. "There'll be another crew along in a few minutes to check on your carpet."

"That's fine," Edgar said. He showed them where they could park their truck nearer the kitchen and left them to their work.

Edgar joined Marcella in the garden with two glasses of iced tea, which he had poured on his way through the kitchen. "Your roses are looking better," he said.

"All it takes is a little time and a lot of love. And a snip here or there."

"I wish your green thumb was contagious. When I was young, my mother taught me to plant radishes and carrots, but that was the extent of my horticultural life."

"But you had such lovely landscaping in Austin," Marcella said.

"Yes, but that's only because Texas has some wonderful landscape artists and lawn care services."

———

THE GARDEN DOOR OPENED AND THE TALLER OF THE carpenters stepped out.

"Mr. Garrison, you might want to see this."

Edgar took a yellowed envelope from him.

"What is it?" Marcella asked, scooting closer on the bench.

"I didn't open it," the carpenter said. "We found it tacked to a stud inside the wall behind the refrigerator."

Edgar inspected the envelope closely, holding it at different angles to make out barely legible flourishes of exquisitely ornate handwriting. "My dearest Frederick," it said.

"Open it," Marcella said, straining for a better look at the envelope. "Carefully, though. It looks fragile."

"It feels like a linen paper, probably quite expensive at the time," Edgar said.

"Excuse me, I'll get back to work," the carpenter said.

Marcella thanked him and said, "Read it, Edgar. The handwriting is lovely."

The age-stained letter began.

"My dearest Frederick,

I sense that this will be my last day on earth. The frailty that has haunted me since you were a young man in knickers has run its course and so has my physical existence. Because I gave birth to you just three months before my forty-fifth birthday, our years together have been fewer than I wish. At ninety-one years of age, I have outlived most women I've known. As my only child, you should know that your grandfather, my father, dictated in his last will and testament that whatever is left of the inheritance which he left to me, should be yours upon my physical departure. I wish to fulfill that desire, but sadly I must also inform you that within that same document, your grandfather stipulated that none of his fortune should be passed to your son, whom he referred to specifically as Frederick Starnes, Junior.

It tears at the very fiber of my heart to inform you that your grandfather wrote detailed instructions to tell you why he left such a heartless demand regarding your son. His words were, 'No coin of mine shall ever support in any way any person, whether blood of mine or not, who chooses not to toil with the sweat of his brow, the strength of his hands, and the power of his mind to provide for those who shall have found themselves born into his lineage.'

My dear, dear Frederick, I must stand by the terms of my father's will and testament as it pertains to any of his financial resources which are mine through inheritance. My body is tired, but my mind is as capable as it has ever been, and I shall do whatever I wish with my personal fortune. I can assure you that it is sizable, thanks to your father's business acumen. I leave you your grandfather's Connecticut estate as well as accounts and assets totaling just over three million dollars. I leave my personal fortune, that part which is mine because of my seventy-year marriage to your father, to your son and my grandson, Frederick Starnes, Junior.

The cash and assets which make up my grandson's inheritance are significant and should provide a very comfortable lifestyle for him as long as he lives. It is, however, his to do with as he wishes. I have just two requests remaining. My first is that he would go out into the world that is his and make it a better one for him and those who come after him. My second is that when you make this announcement to your son, tell him also that although he cannot see me or touch me, I shall be there dancing alongside him, forever with my hands held high declaring to the world, I am Josephine Anne Starnes and these men are my family.

With love,

Your dearest Mother."

"WHO WAS THIS WONDERFUL WOMAN?" MARCELLA ASKED. "Read it again, please. Read it slowly."

Edgar read the letter again, stopping occasionally to absorb the words.

"Don't you just love Josephine's writing? It's as if I can hear her speaking to her son. She was a bold woman," Marcella said.

Edgar held the letter open in his lap, staring across the lawn into a grove of cedar trees. "I bought this house from

Fred Starnes, Jr., yet I know so little about him. What kind of man is he?"

"I really can't say. He had no relatives in this area that I'm aware of. Seemed quite a loner, I thought. What was he like in your dealings with him over this house?"

"He was quiet and very polite, but in an obliged way," Edgar said. "Not much of a talker. There was an artistic air about him, which may account for his moving back to California. The arts scene doesn't seem to be exactly thriving in Morgan Crossroads."

"He must be one of the Fredericks mentioned in the letter. Perhaps he's Josephine's grandson," Marcella said.

Edgar and Marcella sat back on the curve-backed teakwood bench. Marcella took the letter from Edgar and read it a third time, silently.

"Do you know how to get in touch with Mr. Starnes?" Marcella asked.

"I'm sure I have his phone number or address. Why?"

"Well, don't you think we should let him know that we found this letter?"

"I'm not so sure he wants to know," Edgar said. "After all, it must have been him that buried the letter, and possibly the memories it carried, in the walls of this house." Edgar looked the house over, from the roof to the ground. "Was anyone else involved with Fred Starnes in building the house?"

Marcella thought for a moment, then said that she had no memory of anyone else having been involved. "It all seemed so secretive," she said. "There he was, a total stranger with no known connection to anyone in this area. Then one day trucks and workers showed up and transformed the old Greendyke place into this beautiful home place. Mr. Greendyke had been dead for years, and his children had all moved out of state. Fred Starnes bought the land from one of the grandchildren, then mostly stayed away until the builders had finished."

"How would anyone come to this little community for more than a few minutes without Dora Mae Crawford or someone else finding out his life history?" Edgar asked.

"You know how suspicious Henry is of strangers who come to town and stay for a few days. He once told me that Mr. Starnes had stopped by two or three times for cigarettes or coffee or whatever it was. You should ask Henry about him. To hear him tell it, Mr. Starnes never said a word about his past, his family, or anything else, really. Then one day, he just moved back to California. He left the same way he came, apparently."

CHAPTER EIGHT

B<small>IG</small> B<small>END</small> N<small>ATIONAL</small> P<small>ARK</small>. E<small>VERGLADES</small> N<small>ATIONAL</small> P<small>ARK</small>. Yellowstone. Michigan. North Dakota. British Columbia. Petrified Forest. Banff National Park. Cape Canaveral. The RV at the fuel pump in front of Brown's General Store had been everywhere. Or at least it had, if the stickers plastered across the rear end of it meant anything.

"Are there any tourist attractions in this little town?" a lady with a straw hat and fanny pack asked.

"Perhaps a waterfall or some Indian burial grounds, something like that," a silver-haired man with a goatee and brown knee socks added.

Henry Brown rubbed his chin. His eyes took on a deep, searching look. "Some people say they've found arrow heads and such further up in the valley," Henry said, pointing with his thumb. "Henshaw crossing's up that way, too. That's a swimming hole. Haven't been up there in years, but it's still there as far as I know."

"Anything else?" the lady asked. "I have no clue how my husband managed to get us here, but he did. So we may as well act like tourists while we're here."

Henry snapped his fingers as if to welcome a bright idea. "I just remembered, we do have a quilt museum. It's not huge. In fact, the whole thing fits in the front room of Dora Mae Crawford's house."

The man and woman looked at each other. "How do we get there?"

Henry suggested they go out on the porch so they could better see where he was sending them. "Just go through the light and when you come to the third street, hook a left. Dora Mae lives all the way at the end. White house with red shutters and a green roof. Looks like a Christmas house. Just pull right on up in her driveway when you get there. She won't mind a bit."

The RV squeaked its way onto the street and headed toward the third street on the left.

Ollie Smith shook his finger at Henry. "You're not pickled quite right. You know that?"

"Why would he let Dora Mae loose on poor innocent people like them?" Grumpy asked.

"POLLY, LET ME SPEAK TO HENRY."

"Is this Dora Mae?" Polly asked.

"You know who this is. Now, can you put Henry on the phone? I don't care if he's in bed. This is important."

"You realize it's almost ten o'clock don't you?" Polly gave the phone to Henry but held her ear near the receiver.

Dora Mae blazed on, hardly taking a breath. "Henry Brown, do you know that I had to listen to those people telling me every detail of every place they visited in that raggedy old rattle trap of an RV for the last twenty years? You're not going to believe this, but I had to feed them some of my double fried chicken and persimmon pie before they'd ever leave. Would you believe I walked them out on the porch and that lady turned herself around and went right back inside? Said she needed a drink of water.

"They kept asking about some quilt museum, said you told them there was one in my house. And worse than that, they drove that motorhome thing right up in my driveway and parked it there, knowing good and well that I like to have an open view of the mailbox. I like to see when my romance novel of the week comes in. You realize I get one every week, don't you?

"I told those people I make it my business to be aware of whatever is going on in this town, and if there was a quilt museum in my house or anybody else's, I'd be the second to know about it and the first one to tell it.

"What do you have to say for–"

Henry quietly hung up the phone.

"You should be ashamed of yourself, Henry Brown," Polly said, then doubled over laughing.

MARCELLA LOOKED AT THE SKY THROUGH HER KITCHEN window. "Can you believe what a beautiful day it is?" According to the weather reports from the Huntsville television stations, a moderate temperature and low humidity had combined to make the frizz factor the lowest it had been in weeks. It was a perfect day for a trip to Polly's.

It was shaping up to be a big hair day in the beauty shop. Big because most of the regulars had shown up as if they had conspired to overwhelm Polly and her shampoo girl. But big also because every woman in the shop except Stella had hair that had been teased into shapes that were several times larger than the head that grew the hair.

Marcella was recounting the story of her plumbing woes to Jewell Crabtree and the Pearle twins when Dora Mae blew in the door finishing a sentence she had started when she was still alone on the sidewalk.

"Did you hear what Henry did to me? Well, I hope not. I'm so angry I can't even talk about it. He sent not one, but two perfect strangers to my door step. I'm just livid about it."

Jewell said, "I thought you couldn't talk about it."

"I can't. I don't remember the last time I was this mad."

"Well, maybe you shouldn't discuss it," Polly said. "Remember your blood pressure, sweetie."

"They said they'd been everywhere, but I'm not so sure about that. That skinny little man—there wasn't enough of him to hold up one of my irises—he told me they'd even been to Green Bay, Wisconsin."

"I'd love to go to Green Bay," Marcella said.

"Well, don't follow that guy. I just didn't have the heart to tell him that Green Bay was in Illinois, not Wisconsin. Where'd he ever get that idea?" Dora Mae asked.

Polly's hands froze with Marcella's hair stretched straight up, poised for curlers. Marcella's mouth twitched as she avoided snickering. Jewell Crabtree turned her head, choking back a giggle. Stella shook her head as if to say, "Poor thing."

"If Henry Brown ever pulls a stunt like that on me again, I'm just going to kill him."

"Oh, I don't think I'd go that far," one of the Pearle twins said.

"Polly might need him for something," the other twin said.

"I hope this doesn't sound dumb, but I don't understand

what this is that you can't talk about," Jewell said. "And what two people are you going on about?"

The UPS man hopped in, left a package, and hopped back out, but not before he spotted Marcella. "Mrs. Peabody. I have two packages for you. Neiman Marcus this time, I think."

"Great. I've been waiting for them. Edgar's home. He can sign for them."

"Does the UPS man know you're a Garrison now?" one twin asked.

"Yes, but he forgets."

"What two people?" Jewell asked, louder this time.

"She took a breath, honey. Let's not get her started again," Polly said.

CHAPTER NINE

Linda Cruz glanced at the clock over the front door of the pharmacy. Ten o'clock. The air conditioning service company had promised that someone would be there no later than eleven.

The building was built in the early 1950s and updated twenty-five years ago. Apparently, energy efficiency had not been a goal during that renovation. At least it hadn't if the way the building heated in the summer and cooled in the winter were any sign.

First it was the small refrigerator that Linda used to keep water bottles and her lunch cold. When it stopped working she'd added a reminder to the bottom of her to-do list to buy a new one. But when the air conditioner took an unauthorized vacation right in the middle of summer, she decided it was time for another building update.

She'd start first with the air conditioner, then the insulation. There was that awning over the front window and the walls needed paint. And she was growing tired of the ancient floor tiles and the toilet fixtures that looked as though they'd been there as long as the building.

Just before eleven, a white service truck stopped in front of the store. A young man with a clipboard opened the heavy wood and glass front door, hesitating to look up at the jangling bell.

"It's been a long time since I've seen one of those," he said with his thumb pointing over his shoulder.

"It's been there longer than I can remember," Linda said. "Can I help you?"

"I was hoping I could help you. I'm Jason. I'm here to check your air conditioning."

If I'd known air conditioning men looked like you, I'd have called one a long time ago.

"Miss? Your air conditioning?"

"Oh. I'm so sorry. I was thinking about something. It's out back. I'll show you." She motioned for him to follow her.

After a couple trips to retrieve tools and testing equipment, Jason stopped trekking through the store and settled in to work on the air unit.

The bell over the door announced the Pearle twins' arrival. "We need a bottle of rubbing alcohol and a scouring pad," one of them said.

"She spilled a bottle of bright red finger nail polish," the other one said.

"I didn't spill it. It slipped out of my hand."

"Well, whether it spilled or the bottle slipped, there is still red polish all over my side of the bathroom counter top."

Linda directed them to the alcohol. "Are you sure you should use scouring pads on your counter top?"

"Oh," the first one said. "Those are for the pan that she used to burn the meatloaf last night."

"Pay her no attention, Linda. She'll have you believing I burned the meatloaf intentionally."

Jason stepped from the back room and ignored the twins on his way to the front door.

Linda and the twins watched him leave the store and open the back doors of his van. For what seemed like several minutes, he stayed in one position with his top half bent over into his van.

"What else have you hidden away back there?" the second twin asked.

"Nothing. Nobody," Linda said. "He's just here to work on the air conditioning."

"Where is he from?" the first twin asked.

"Huntsville."

"Well, I'd keep my eye on him if I were you," the first twin said.

"I would, too," the second twin said. "I'm not sure men had muscles like that when we were your age."

"You should be ashamed of yourself. You know very well that you were nearly beside yourself every time you saw a muscle twitch," the first twin said.

"With arms and shoulders like those I sure wouldn't want that one to get away," the second one said.

The twins left with their alcohol and scouring pads, and both winked as they pulled the door shut.

Linda took a makeup mirror from the display and looked to see if her face was as red as it felt.

"WHAT WOULD YOU RECOMMEND FOR AN ANTIHISTAMINE?" THE man in blue jeans and a plaid shirt asked.

"Don't I know you?" Linda Cruz asked.

"Maybe. When I was in high school, your uncle would pay me to wash his windows and clean up the store."

"That's right," Linda said. "You're Todd Jenkins, the one he kept telling me about."

"How did you remember my name?"

"Because he would use your full name every time he talked about you. 'Todd Jenkins sure does a nice job on my windows.' Or, 'Did you know that Todd Jenkins makes straight A's in chemistry class?' I heard your name every time I saw my uncle."

Todd's eyebrows scrunched. "Why would he tell you about me?"

"I can't say. Maybe he just thought you were a nice guy. Oh, you asked for antihistamine," she said, hurrying to the allergy section two aisles over. "This is good. You don't have high blood pressure, do you?"

He shook his head.

"Then this one should be fine. Is there anything else I can help you find?"

He turned his eyes downward as if surveying the pattern on the counter. Then he looked up. "Actually, I heard you had a little refrigerator that wasn't cooling right. I do refrigeration work and wonder if I might help you with it."

"Who told you that my refrigerator needed repair?"

"Oh, some lady I saw in Haley's Grocery this morning."

This is strange. "Well, it's not cooling like it should. But I haven't decided whether to repair it or replace it. And there's already an air conditioning man here. He's working out back. That's his truck out there," she said, pointing toward the window.

"That's all right. I didn't know you'd called anyone already," he said. He held up his bag of antihistamine. "Thanks for the advice."

"Hey, Todd," she said as she reached for note paper and a

pen. "Give me your phone number and I'll think about that refrigerator."

———

Marcella served herself a slice of Eva Jo's Dutch apple pie.

"Coffee?" Eva Jo asked as she poured a cup for herself. "Fresh pot."

Marcella held her cup toward the pot. "Thank you."

"I want you to look out there," Eva Jo said. She pointed through the screen door to a garden that looked large enough for a neighborhood. "See that row of okra?"

"What about it?"

"It's about to wear me out, that's what. See that washtub on the counter?" She pointed across the room. "That one by the fridge. All of that came from one row. I can't cut it fast enough."

"If you need to get rid of some of it, I can take some to Edgar. He loves it any way I cook it," Marcella said.

"Take him a sack of it. Tomatoes, too. I can't can them fast enough. Between the okra and the tomatoes, that garden's a full-time job. Pick through and take him the young okra. Those big ones might be too tough to suit him."

Marcella took the old envelope from her purse. "Read this," she said, sliding it across the table.

"What is it? One of your old love letters?"

"No. Just read it. Handle the paper carefully, though."

Eva Jo read the letter, then more slowly she read some lines again. "Who is this Josephine lady?"

"I believe she's Mr. Starnes's grandmother," Marcella said. "But I'm not sure I have the generations correct.

"First off, where did you find this?" Eva Jo asked.

"The men who repaired the kitchen found it tacked to some wood inside the wall."

"Why would it be in there? And who would have put it there?"

"I'd say it had to be Fred Starnes, or perhaps he had the carpenters hide it for him when they built the house," Marcella said.

"Do you think the Fred we know was one of the fellas in that letter? That's a lot of Fredericks, you know."

"Edgar and I talked about that. We believe he's Josephine's grandson."

"Whoever that old man in that letter is, he sounds like an ornery old goat. I just don't think the two of us would have gotten along. Good for Josephine, though, speaking her mind," Eva Jo said.

"Did you ever meet Fred Starnes?" Marcella asked.

"No, other than that day in Haley's Grocery. The two of us said we were sorry when we ran our shopping carts head-on into each other. Made him drop a box of raisin bran right there in the middle of the aisle."

"Did he seem like a nice man? Was he gentle spirited or gruff?"

"Now we can't judge people on just one little shopping cart accident, but I'd say . . ." Eva Jo clasped her hands and rolled her eyes toward the ceiling in a prayerful posture. "I'd say he was a quiet sort of man. He looked like he could get right with a person if he thought he needed to, but you couldn't have told that by his voice. Almost meek, I'd say."

"I wonder why he never took the time or initiative to meet any of us on a personal level," Marcella said. "I don't remember ever seeing him in Lucy's or even the Post Office, come to think of it." She slid her chair back and poured herself a fresh cup of coffee at the counter.

"I'll take a little shot, too," Eva Jo said, sliding her cup toward Marcella. "Are you sure he even lived in that house? I mean, did he really live in it? Like sleeping and eating there?"

"I'm not sure about that. But I used to drive by and daydream about living in such a house. He must have contracted someone to keep up the landscaping. It was always perfectly manicured. It looked so much like those I'd seen in *House Beautiful* magazine."

"Now look at yourself," Eva Jo said, holding her hands out as if presenting Marcella to the world.

"Oh my, I nearly fainted the day Edgar drove me to the house and showed me the inside. He asked if I would like to live there after our wedding. I nearly melted when he asked me that question," Marcella said.

"Then he hauled off and bought it for you," Eva Jo said over laughter. "Best I ever got from any of my husbands was a trip to the drive-in movie."

"Eva Jo, do you know what the most peculiar thing about the house was? It looked like a model home. As if they never intended it to be a full-time residence like it is for Edgar and me."

"Well, reckon why the guy had it built? If I remember right, he was from California or Oregon or somewhere out that direction."

"California, I think. I've wondered the same thing, though. As far as I can tell, he had no relatives in this area and no job. So why would he build a fine home like that out here in this valley?"

"And what does Fred Starnes do for a living? That's what I want to know. He sure didn't build that house on milking money. You reckon he could even milk a cow?" Eva Jo laughed her way to the refrigerator. "How about some ice cream?"

"These have got to be the best pancakes I've had today," Henry Brown said. "How about a couple more to go with this coffee?"

"Looks like you might need more bacon, too. Or maybe a slice of ham." Stella said.

"Okay, but don't tell Polly."

Stella winked. "Which one, bacon or ham?"

"Surprise me."

Stella headed for the kitchen and stopped to refill Lorraine Haley's coffee cup on the way.

"Mind if I join you?" the voice behind Henry said.

"Edgar! You bet," Henry said, pointing to the other seats. "There's only one of me, but four chairs, so take your pick. Marcella's not eating breakfast?"

"She stayed up late last night working on an article for *The Whipper County Gazette* and woke up this morning with a headache. I think she's trying to sleep it off. I looked around the kitchen and decided that I'd have to come here if I was going to have a decent breakfast."

"Dora Mae been hounding her again?" Henry asked.

"You might call it that. Marcella said she called demanding an article by morning. Dora Mae never accepted that she was more than a week early."

"They ought to call that little paper the Whipper County Grapevine. Once in a while Dora Mae will mess up and write something worth reading. Except for stuff Marcella writes, most of it's just gossip, though. What's Marcella writing about this month?"

"I don't know if she went with the suggestion, but Dora Mae insisted on an article about the history of quilting in Morgan Crossroads. That seems like an odd request of a person who normally writes about gardening, grammar rules, and fashion."

"Well, old buddy, you haven't been around too very long but I think you'll eventually find this out on your own. There are days that Dora Mae's elevator doesn't quite make it to the top floor, if you know what I mean."

"She seems like a nice lady," Edgar said. "A little loud at times, but still polite."

"Oh, she's usually nice," Henry said. "She'd do anything in the world for a person. That is until she gets a burr under her saddle about something. It's easy to get her all stirred up."

"You don't suppose this article request stems from a conversation someone had about a quilt museum, do you?"

"You said you needed some breakfast," Henry said. "Try the pancakes. She's doing them just right this morning."

"I think I'd better stay away from that side of the menu. Diabetes and pancake syrup can't seem to get along," Edgar said.

"Stella serves a mean omelet, too. Here she comes. She'll sure fix you up. Watch this."

Stella topped off Henry's coffee. "How about you, Edgar? What are you having this morning?

"Bring him one of those kitchen sink omelets," Henry said. "You know, the one with two or three kinds of meat, cheese, and peppers and onions. My treat. No jelly, though. He's diabetic, remember?"

Stella raised a questioning eyebrow toward Edgar.

"That will be just fine. Thank you," Edgar said.

CHAPTER TEN

"I've been thinking," Ollie Smith said.

"Run for cover, everybody!" Grumpy said as he jumped up from his rocking chair.

Henry Brown and Cecil Grey covered their heads as if the roof over the Brown's General Store porch might fall on them.

"The last time I heard you say that, you blew about half the roof off of your hay barn," Grumpy said.

"Well, that woulda never happened if somebody'd told me they'd left a case of shotgun shells out there."

"Wasn't me," Cecil said.

"What was it you've been thinking about?" Henry asked.

Just then, Edgar eased his BMW off the highway, barely making a noise on the gravel. Every eye on the porch followed his arrival as if the men had expected him.

"Boy, am I glad to see you," Ollie said. "For a minute I thought I might need a lawyer to settle these fellows down a bit."

"Are they ganging up on you again?" Edgar asked.

"Like flies on a picnic," Ollie said.

Bull threw his hands up, palms out. "Not guilty."

"Same here." Grumpy patted his chest.

"I just work here," Henry said.

Ollie leaned forward in his chair. "Edgar, you tell me what you think of this idea. Lately, the women around here've been conniving and sneaking around, having their fancy shindigs."

"Yep, and you watch them," Grumpy said. "You can ask them what they're up to and they'll just stare you in the eye, like you've dreamed up the most ridiculous question ever asked."

"Well, I've been thinking about that. I think us fellows need to knock our heads together and come up with a shindig of our own," Ollie said.

"Have you ever planned a shindig before?" Edgar asked.

"Maybe not altogether by myself, but I did help come up the idea for that wedding party we threw for you and Marcella over there in Lucy's parking lot."

"That was your idea?" Edgar asked.

"Maybe not all of it," Ollie said. "It was my idea to throw some wieners on the grill in case anybody was there that didn't care too much for steaks and such."

"What's your idea this time?" Cecil Grey asked.

"I've been thinking about our little community park over there." Ollie pointed across the street in the general direction of the park a block behind Lassiter's Laundromat. "It's starting to look pathetic, if you ask me. Those flower beds haven't been tended to in months. The picnic tables look like Saint Peter and those fellows might've used them at the last supper. And you know what I noticed? That sorry little softball field is still there, but there's not a single place where two people can play a game of horseshoes. The grass is so tall that if you was to throw yourself a ringer, you'd never know it."

"And that old barbecue grill, if you could call it that, is plumb rusted out on the bottom," Grumpy said.

"So what's your idea?" Edgar asked.

"We need a new horseshoe pit and a new barbecue grill. Grumpy, I bet you could weld up a good stout one to put out there," Ollie said.

"I'd sure like to see a covered picnic area or two," Cecil said. "Years ago we had community-wide picnics in that park, but we just kinda let life take them away from us."

"Abe would probably tear into those flower beds for us, like he does those up and down Main," Grumpy said.

"We'd have to think of some way to raise the money for all that stuff. I don't think we could keep it near as big a secret as them women do," Ollie said.

"I don't know the first thing about building picnic tables and barbecue grills. And I've never played horseshoes," Edgar said.

"Well, we can fix that," Henry said.

"But I'd be willing to help with the planning and cooking."

Ollie held up an index finger. "First thing is, we've gotta do some kind of fundraising event. I've been thinking maybe we could get some country singer or one of those gospel groups, whoever we can get. We could sell tickets and maybe raffle off some stuff," Ollie said.

"How about a gigantic yard sale, one of those that could draw people from Huntsville and all over," Cecil said.

"Just don't have it on a First Monday weekend. If we do, everybody will be over in Scottsboro roaming around the square looking at everything from mules to knitting needles instead of here in Morgan Crossroads," Henry said.

"Is there enough junk in this town to have a sale like that?

I mean, we'd need enough stuff to handle the crowd," Grumpy said.

"Polly's hoarded enough junk away in our attic to stock a good sized sale on her own," Henry said.

"How about asking Eva Jo?" Cecil asked. "Last time I was up in her barn loft, there was so much stuff up there that I couldn't believe it. I'm talking furniture, old appliances that I imagine are antique and collectable by now. And who knows what else?"

"Well, how about it everybody? Is a fix up the park fundraiser a good idea?" Ollie asked.

"Well, the only thing I know is, that's a heck of a lot better idea than your other one," Grumpy said. "And there's no ammunition involved."

MARCELLA PHONED JESSE. "WE'RE LOOKING FORWARD TO having you here. Your father and I will meet you at the airport in Huntsville. Okay. We love you, too. Goodbye."

"When is he coming?" Edgar asked.

"Thursday of next week."

"I didn't hear you say anything about why you invited him."

"What do you mean? I told him we've missed him and would like to see him again soon."

"Is it the attorney in me, or is there a fly on the wall somewhere telling me you might also want everyone to see your entry in the contest for Linda Cruz's affections?" Edgar asked with a grin in one corner of his mouth.

"Contest. What contest?" Marcella hoped the heat in her cheeks wasn't visible. "It would be nice, I suppose, if Jesse were to meet Linda again."

"Again?"

"I'm sure they must've met at our wedding. Don't you think they did? They were both there."

"Oh. I suppose they might remember each other. How are you going to arrange this meeting?"

"I have no plans of arranging a meeting. But I'm sure it will happen."

"Would you like some privileged information?" Edgar asked.

"Sure, as long as it isn't gossip. I heard enough of that at the beauty shop this morning. I love every woman in this community, but I wonder how they come up with some of the stories they tell."

"Well, my dear, this isn't gossip. I witnessed this myself. Somebody else has already entered their contestant in the race."

Marcella straightened herself and closed the home decorating catalog she'd been mindlessly thumbing through. "Who?"

"I was in the pharmacy a few days ago when a young man came in and asked for some little something. Linda found whatever it was and asked what else he needed. It turns out that he was there because he'd run into some lady in the grocery store who told him Linda's refrigerator might need repair. She said he should hurry over there to see if he could help her with it."

"Did he describe her?"

"No, he said nothing about that. I don't think he got very far with Linda."

"Good."

"What does that mean? I thought there was no contest," he said, drawing her to him for a gentle shoulder hug.

"Can I ask just one tiny favor of you?" Marcella asked.

"Ask anything you wish, Dear. I'm all ears."

"Do you think I could ask Linda to join the two of us and Jesse for a nice dinner at Lucy's one evening?"

"I think we can manage that."

OLLIE WROTE OUT WHAT HE WANTED TO SAY AND HAD HIS WIFE proofread it. Then, he took a copy that he had written with a black marker to the office at Morgan Chapel where Lucille ran off fifty copies. She did so only after he agreed to leave a donation in the box by the front door to cover the paper cost.

"Attention Morgan Crossroads," the flyer began. "The men are putting together a fundraiser to help us fix up the park. Huge yard sale (exact location of the yard to be determined). Barbecue and special entertainment (if we can get anybody to agree to do it). Take your yard sale donations to Grumpy's Garage. Cakes and pies might be good, too. Take them to Henry Brown at the store (but not until the day before the event)."

Ollie and Cecil spent half the day driving around, tacking flyers on telephone poles and taping them up in store front windows at Lucy's Cafe, Haley's Grocery, and Brown's General Store. The hardware store in Porterville agreed to host a flyer if the men promised to buy at least some project supplies there. Lassiter's Laundromat promised thirty days of free washing and twenty-five cent dryers to the first ten customers who donated at least twenty-five dollars to the cause. The Dairy Bar offered a free ice cream cone for each ten-dollar donation.

Jeremiah Downs allowed Edgar to post one on the announcement board in the vestibule at Morgan Chapel.

CHAPTER ELEVEN

MID-MORNING ON WEDNESDAY, MICHAEL PARKED HIS grandmother's pickup truck with its rusty bed filled with ladders and tools in front of Crossroads Pharmacy. He surveyed the place where the awning had been before it fell.

He opened the front door and held it for Marcella as she came out carrying a new glucometer for Edgar.

"Thank you," she said. "Working on the awning?"

"I'm going to give it my best shot," Michael said.

He watched Marcella drive her old Chevy away, around the corner with no attention at all to the stop sign or to Grumpy, whose sudden stop saved her fender and his.

Linda met Michael half-way along the main aisle. "How are you feeling?"

"Fine, I feel great. Why are you asking?"

"Eva Jo was in here not too long ago picking up some bandages. She said you'd had an accident of some kind."

"Oh, that," he said, waving it off. "I slid down a hill with my bike, but I'm over that now."

"Great. What can I do for you?"

Granny said that you needed help with your awning. I thought maybe I could take a look at it.

"Sure. Let's do that," Linda said.

The two of them went first to the storage room behind the building where her uncle had hidden the awning, then to the sidewalk to survey the damage.

"Do you think you can do it by yourself?" Linda asked.

"I think so. If I see that I need help, I'll go round up somebody."

"My uncle could probably help you hold it in place. I can call him if you need me to."

A mousy sounding horn tooted as a small red car crawled past in front of the store.

Michael turned to watch it drive away. "Who was that?"

"Dora Mae Crawford, I think," Linda said.

Michael worked to reinstall the drugstore awning. Over a period of three hours, he watched the same red compact car creep past four times.

MARCELLA SAT IN HER FAVORITE QUEEN ANNE CHAIR READING an Agatha Christie novel. Across the side table from her, a slight rumble rose and fell as Edgar snored in his recliner. A Pat Conroy novel lay closed in his lap.

She reached across the table and rubbed his arm. "Edgar?"

He raised the back of the recliner and attempted to answer as if he had been wide awake. "Yes, Dear. What do you need? A glass of tea?"

"No, I don't need anything. I've been thinking about that letter."

"Have you read it again?"

"No, not in the past few days. I think we should try to contact Mr. Starnes."

"Are you sure that's a good idea?" Edgar asked.

"On the surface, perhaps not. But in my heart, I have a burning feeling that we should try to call him. Maybe we can invite him back here to spend a few days with us," Marcella said.

"What do you think that would accomplish?"

"Perhaps nothing would come of it. But there is also a possibility that he needs someone to invite him into their life. What do you think?"

"I don't know about that. From what I understand, he was a very private person."

"That's what I've heard. But what if he really doesn't want to be like that? What if he's lonely?"

"Oh, Marcella. I don't think we should invite him here with any ulterior motive to change him."

"Nor do I," Marcella said. "But I know what loneliness is and I think he may, as well."

Edgar took Marcella's hand in his and looked deep into the blue of her eyes. "When would you like to invite him?"

"Soon. The sooner the better, in fact."

"I'll look over the documents from the closing and see if I can locate him," Edgar said. "But please, don't expect a welcoming response."

"I won't. But I'll be thrilled if he gives us one."

Marcella started toward the kitchen. "I'm going to check the pantry. I'll need to do some grocery shopping. Jesse will be here tomorrow, and then Mr. Starnes. This will be so much fun."

As she walked, Edgar noticed that she seemed to glow for a moment, as if the red in her hair had brightened and a twinkle had somehow lit the room.

MARCELLA PARKED HER OLD CHEVY PARTLY ON THE GRASS beside Eva Jo's front porch.

"Drag up a chair," Eva Jo said, pointing to one near her. "And grab a lap full of beans while you're at it. Snap a sack full for Edgar. Does he like green beans?"

"He loves them," Marcella said. Her eyebrows scrunched as she studied her fingernails.

"As perfect as those nails are, they'll survive a few beans. You might have to get Polly to repaint them, but they'll pull through," Eva Jo said.

"Honey, I just had them done yesterday. Do you suppose I can pass on the bean snapping for now?"

"I reckon, but you still have to take a sack full to Edgar. What brings you out here? You've got a look on your face like you just won the lottery or something. What's going on?"

"I need a couple pies and a cake or two," Marcella said.

Eva Jo's hands dropped to her lap with a bean mid-snap. "Don't tell me you're trying to throw Edgar into a diabetic tizzy."

"When can you bake them? I think I'd like one of your big pecan pies, an apple pie with that lovely lattice work that you do so well, and a lemon meringue."

"Is that all? That's only a day's work," Eva Jo said, waving it off with one hand.

"I think we'll need about three cakes, too."

"At the same time? Honey, you surely don't mean at the same time."

"Well, no," Marcella said. "I could pick up the pies one day and the cakes the next."

"If I do all that baking for you, who's going to do the

milking and the feeding? And who's gonna fetch the eggs from the hen house?"

"Oh, you should have plenty of time for that, shouldn't you?" Marcella asked. "Maybe Michael would be willing to help you."

"What kind of cakes are you hoping to get out of me?"

"I thought one of your beautiful pineapple upside down cakes–the ones with the deliciously gooey syrup and pineapple rings on top. I don't know how you do it. I've tried to bake upside down cakes before and they flop every time."

"What else?" Eva Jo asked.

"I really should have another one of those diabetic cakes like the one you baked for Edgar's birthday. And I like chocolate. German chocolate would be nice. Can you do that for me?"

"I'll have to–"

"You know I'd be happy to pay for all the ingredients and whatever you need for your time and effort," Marcella said.

"When do you need these masterpieces?" Eva Jo asked.

"I'd love to at least have the pecan pie tomorrow."

"Tomorrow! Honey, you know I love you like a sister, but that is cutting it close, don't you think?"

"Please. Jesse is flying into Huntsville tomorrow afternoon and he loves pecan pie."

"Have you ever considered becoming a sales person? I bet you could persuade Ollie Smith to trade in his John Deere tractor for a mule," Eva Jo said, laughing.

"I'm on my way to Haley's. There are so many things I need to pick up."

"I don't remember Jesse eating that much."

Marcella held up both hands with crossed fingers. "We hope we'll have another house guest, too."

"Really? Who might that be?" Eva Jo asked.

"Fred Starnes."

Eva Jo jerked, sending the bowl of snapped beans onto the floor.

Marcella bent to help pick up the beans.

"Did you say Fred Starnes? The one Edgar bought your house from?"

"The very one," Marcella said.

"Why is he coming back to Morgan Crossroads?"

"I'm not positive he's coming, but I feel sure he will after Edgar spends a little time on the phone with him."

"Is this about that letter?"

"Partly, I suppose," Marcella said. "But it's really about Mister Starnes. I do so hope he comes. It will be such a joy to have the two of them here at the same time."

"So, Edgar plans to call him?"

"If he can find his telephone number. Edgar's really an expert at looking up things that most people might find difficult."

"What are you going to do if he refuses to come?"

"I thought about that, but I really believe he'll come. I'm so eager to learn more about him and his family."

"As private as he was when he lived here, I'd have to consider it a minor miracle if Edgar even gets him to answer the phone," Eva Jo said.

"I haven't told Edgar about this, but I had a dream last night."

"About Edgar?"

"No, not directly. I dreamed about the Starnes family. You know that I've never been to an opera or to a classical music concert."

"I didn't know you ever wanted to go," Eva Jo said.

"When I was young, I wanted to be a glamorous actress.

But I remember listening to classical music when my father would play it on that old Victrola that his mother had passed down—the one that's in my sitting room. And I've seen operas on public television."

"Where does Fred Starnes come into all this?"

"In my dream, his mother was an elegant opera star who could at a moment's notice become the most exciting concert pianist. And Fred was a ballet dancer whose movements were the most graceful ever. He danced in a way that made him seem almost non-human, the way he would glide across the stage."

"I don't know much about that kind of dancing and singing." Eva Jo chuckled. "I can talk to you about the Grand Ole Opry, but I don't know a thing about all that fancy singing and dancing. What does that dream have to do with anything?"

Marcella lit up. "What if Mister Starnes comes to Morgan Crossroads and we find that he really has those talents? What if he actually is a ballet dancer, or maybe a concert pianist?"

Eva Jo shrugged.

"I think it would be wonderful if we could persuade him to do a concert or recital for us. Maybe we could use the hall in Morgan Chapel or even the school auditorium if we could interest enough people."

"I don't know about that," Eva Jo said. "I'm not trying to mess up your dream. But I just can't see too many people in this valley being willing to sit still for an hour or two while a man that nobody knows flits across the stage or plays some kind of fancy music that they've never heard of."

"Eva Jo! You would be surprised to find out the number of people in this area who would love to spend time doing something completely different from anything they've ever done. And it would be such fun."

"I sure hope you don't come out disappointed, Honey. What if this Starnes guy can't dance or play anything but a radio like the rest of us?" Eva Jo asked.

"Then we'll just learn from him, whatever he can teach us."

CHAPTER TWELVE

"I'M TELLING YOU, SOMETHING'S GOING ON UP AT THE drugstore," Dora Mae Crawford drawled with her head laid back in the sink at the washing station.

"Like what?" Jewell Crabtree asked.

"I don't know exactly."

"Well, describe it," Polly said.

"I can't. There's enough to look suspicious, but not enough to get any real idea what's going on," Dora Mae said.

"I guess you know you're making about zero sense," Eva Jo, who was there for her monthly do up, said.

"How do you know something's going on," Jewell asked.

"I saw it, that's how."

"Saw what?" Eva Jo asked.

"Eva Jo Clomper, you're just trying to start something," Dora Mae said.

If there was anything Eva Jo hated, it was being called by her full name. She'd hated it since she was a girl and her mother called out to her, "Eva Jo Clomper, you'd better get an iron ahold of that blouse before you wear it." Or, "Eva Jo Clomper, if you don't stop tracking mud in this kitchen, I'm gonna sic your daddy on you." Eva Jo tried to ignore Dora Mae whenever she used that name, considering she had been cursed with a short memory. One that was short enough she didn't remember the eleven-year-old Eva Jo holding her face down in the school yard and tying her hair in knots that took the teacher and a pair of scissors to eliminate.

"I heard you've been doing slow-motion trips past the drug store snooping on Linda Cruz," Polly said.

"That's what I heard, too," Eva Jo said. "If you're going to sneak around, you need to do it in something a little less obvious than a bright red car."

"I've not been snooping," Dora Mae said.

"What would you call it?" Jewell asked.

"It's my duty to keep up with what's going on in Morgan Crossroads. How else would you expect me to come up with enough news to fill a paper?"

The Pearle twins walked in right in the middle of Dora Mae's plea for reason. "I think it would be nice to have some real news reported," the first twin said.

"I'd love that, too," the second twin said. "We could have our very own version of *The New York Times*."

"I'd settle for just a plain little paper with some substance to it," Polly said. "Marcella writes about the only thing worth reading in that little *Gazette*."

"Ladies, you have completely derailed my conversation," Dora Mae said.

"Okay, let's all be quiet," Jewell said.

"Try again," Polly said, holding her hand out as if yielding the floor.

"There were three men in the drugstore on the same day. I mean on the very same day. Now that was no coincidence."

"I'm confused. Has Linda Cruz started serving ladies only?" the first twin asked.

"No, I don't suppose so," Dora Mae said.

"Then why would it be such a strange thing for three men to go in the drugstore on the same day?" Jewell asked.

"These weren't your average everyday men. They were all good looking muscular young men. Not one of them was over thirty, I'd say."

Polly laughed. "What? Are you saying we only have ugly men around here?"

"No, no. I am most certainly not saying that."

"Well, who were they?"

"One of them was that Jenkins boy. He was okay, though. I saw him in Haley's Grocery and suggested he might pick up a few extra dollars by repairing Linda's refrigerator," Dora Mae said. "But the others–"

"I know what Dora Mae was doing. She was snooping around to be sure her fellow had no competition in the race for Linda," the second Pearle twin said.

"I did no such thing."

"Who were the other guys?" Polly asked.

"One of them was a stranger working on something behind the building," Dora Mae said. "He was a keeper, too. Looked like a thirty-year-old Paul Bunyan. I think he had more muscles than he was supposed to have, though."

"How was it that you managed to plant yourself in all the right places so you could gather all that information?"

"I'm observant," Dora Mae said. "A reporter has to be quick with her eye."

"And the other one was?" Jewell prodded with her hands.

"That grandson of Eva Jo's, what's his name?"

"His name is Michael," Eva Jo said.

"That was him. He was out there on the sidewalk working like a wild man, trying to install an awning over the front window. He had a lot of muscles, too. I'm guessing he must have brought most of them back with him from the Middle East."

"He takes after his granny," Eva Jo said. "That's where he gets them."

"So, what's the big deal about those young men showing up at the drug store?" the first twin asked.

"I'm sure that Jenkins boy was there to work on Linda's refrigerator and nothing else," Dora Mae said.

"Right. And the pope is a Baptist," Polly said.

Dora Mae drawled on. "Is he? I didn't know that. I thought he was Polish or something. I'll have to put that in the *Gazette*. I have a hunch that one certain granny might have sent one certain grandson over there to make goo-goo eyes at poor Linda."

"Here's what I think," Eva Jo said. "I think Dora Mae was circling the block so she could keep an eye on her horse's performance in the race for Linda's affection."

"Well, the test is, did Linda fall for any of them?" Jewell asked. "That's what I want to know."

"Mind you, I wasn't spying or being sneaky. But I didn't see a single sign that anyone had swept Linda Cruz off her feet." Dora Mae paused for a moment, looking confused. "What horse?"

"That young fellow asking about the refrigerator, maybe? Well, we'll see who sweeps who off of their feet," Eva Jo said. "But I don't think we should read about it in *The Whipper County Gazette*. That just seems kinda personal, if you ask me."

"WE WOULD BE HAPPY TO HAVE YOU," EDGAR SAID. "YOU HAVE my number. Call me as soon as you have your flight arrangements."

Marcella came into the kitchen and set two bags from Haley's Grocery on the counter. "You would not believe who I…" She clasped her hand over her mouth.

Edgar covered the phone with his hand and said to Marcella, "It's Fred Starnes."

Marcella clinched two shaking hands across her chest. A smile took over her face.

"Okay, Fred," Edgar said. "Don't worry about renting a car, I'll be happy to pick you up at the airport, no matter what time the flight arrives."

Edgar hung up the phone.

"You talked to Fred Starnes?" Marcella asked.

"That was him. I'd remember that voice anywhere."

"When is he coming? I'll need to go back to Haley's. I wonder what he likes to eat. Did you ask him?" She glanced around the room. "I'll have to clean this house before he comes."

Edgar touched her cheek with the palm of his hand. "The house is spotless already. It will be fine."

"Did he say what he likes to eat?"

"No, Dear. We didn't get into that. But I feel certain he'll love whatever you offer."

"When is he coming? Tomorrow?"

"On Thursday or Friday," Edgar said.

"Of this week? Oh my, that's so soon. I've got to call Eva Jo. I hope she has my cakes and pies baked by then." Marcella froze. "Thursday? Edgar, Jesse's coming in on Thursday, too. Oh, my–"

"We'll be fine. Try to relax, Dear. We have plenty of

bedrooms and more bathrooms than we know what to do with."

"But we'll have to eat, and what if I burn dinner?" Marcella asked.

"You won't. I can help you with breakfast. Eva Jo always comes through for you. She'll have your cakes and pies by then. We can eat out or have Stella pack food for carry out."

Marcella leaned on Edgar. "I just want to make a good impression on Mr. Starnes."

"Then just be yourself. There is no better impression that you could make than that."

CHAPTER THIRTEEN

"HERE'S WHAT I THINK," OLLIE SMITH SAID TO THREE OTHER whittlers and spitters at Brown's General Store. "If as many people come in here as I think there could be, we might find ourselves with a big problem on our hands."

"What's that?" Grumpy asked.

"Not enough wieners to feed 'em," Cecil said. "Or grills to cook them on."

"Nope, that's not it. We'll have plenty of wieners and hamburgers and such."

"Okay, let's see," Henry said. "Not enough junk to sell at the yard sale."

"That's not it either. And by the way, it's not a junk sale. It's a sale of the finest no longer wanted stuff in north Alabama," Ollie said.

"Can't be but one other thing," Grumpy said. "Nobody here can count that much money, if you don't include Edgar, that is."

"I think we can get the money counted," Henry said.

"It's traffic control. We've never had so many cars coming

into Morgan Crossroads at one time, except maybe for that shindig we threw when Edgar and Marcella got married."

Henry looked around. "We don't have much in the way of parking lots, but we have plenty of streets to park on. And they can always park on the grass at the park if it don't rain."

A little red car pulled to a stop in front of the store.

"It's Dora Mae," Ollie said.

"Well, look here," Henry said. "It's been a long time since you stopped by. What can we do for you?"

"I hear you men have been planning an event of some kind. Is that right?" Dora Mae asked as she removed a notepad and pen from her purse.

"Event seems like a fancy word for it, but we might come up with one, if things go right."

"Well, you know that I'll need to run that in *The Whipper County Gazette*. That is, if it's not something that might embarrass the community."

"As a matter of fact, you can do us a big favor," Ollie said.

"I came here to get the facts for a story," Dora Mae said.

"When did the facts become anything important in that paper?" Grumpy asked.

Dora Mae ignored the question, except for a look that might have killed a smaller person than Grumpy. "I publish only the facts, to the extent that I can determine them, that is."

"Okay, men, let's come up with some facts for Dora Mae."

"Here's one," Ollie said. "We need stuff to sell at the biggest yard sale ever to be held in these parts."

"How is a yard sale an event?" Dora Mae asked. "Who will it benefit?"

"The community of Morgan Crossroads, Alabama, that's who," Ollie said. "We're having a fund raiser so we can fix up the park. You know, new horseshoe pits, new flowers, and maybe a new ball field if the money stretches that far."

Dora Mae wrote down at least part of what had been said. "And when do you plan to have this fundraiser?"

"We don't know yet. Depends on how much stuff people donate and how long it takes them to do it," Henry said.

Dora Mae dropped her hands to her side. "How am I supposed to write an article about an event you don't even know for sure is going to take place? People around here would think I'd lost the rest of my mind."

"Well, you could just write a practice article and ask people to carry anything they might want to donate to the cause over to Grumpy's garage. He'll hold it in his storage building until we're sure we have enough stuff to call it the biggest yard sale ever to hit north Alabama," Ollie said.

"So you want me to write a practice article so you can practice collecting things for a yard sale that you may or may not have. Is that right?"

"That's pretty close. Be sure to tell them about the hot dogs and hamburgers and the cold drinks and sack races and so on," Ollie said.

Dora scratched a big X across her notes, climbed back into her little red car and drove away.

MARCELLA'S MOST MEMORABLE TIME IN AN AIRPORT HAD BEEN when she, Edgar, and Eva Jo landed in Huntsville on a large private jet after a flight from Texas. The plane had been owned by a friend of Edgar's who agreed to loan it because he owed Edgar a substantial favor. She never asked what the favor was.

It was at the end of that flight that the residents of

Morgan Crossroads got their first glimpse of Edgar Garrison, the tall handsome man whom Marcella had met five decades earlier in a University of Texas library. One might have thought an actor or the president of the United States had shown up, gauging from the reaction when Edgar stepped out of the van.

No one—not even her best friend, Eva Jo—had ever known of Edgar's existence before his son, Jesse, appeared in Marcella's front yard accompanied by his dog, Spotlight. He had hitch-hiked from Texas, hoping to learn more about the lady his adopted dad had spoken so fondly of.

According to the schedule board, Jesse's flight was due to arrive on time. Marcella gripped the elbow of Edgar's sport coat, occasionally rising on her toes, trying to see Jesse. At six feet, eight inches, most of which were covered with tattoos, he would be an imposing figure beside most people. "I don't see him yet."

Edgar searched for a clock and found one above the concourse entrance. "His plane has landed, according to the information board. You should see him in just a few minutes."

"I'm so anxious," Marcella said.

Ten minutes later Edgar said, "There he is. See back there, along the left wall?"

"He's more handsome every time I see him," Marcella said.

"Is he the only one?" Edgar asked with a grin.

"Of course not. You both just grow more handsome with each day," Marcella said.

"Jesse! Jesse," she said, waving her arms. "Over here."

When he saw Marcella and his father, Jesse hurried the last few steps. He bent over and hugged Marcella in a way that was tender and affirming. With a handshake and bear hug, he greeted Edgar.

"You two are getting younger, aren't you?" Jesse asked.

"It's Marcella who's growing younger," Edgar said.

"Well, you both certainly look good. Marriage must be healthy for both of you. Something is, for sure."

"That's enough flattery for now," Marcella said. "Save some for later. You must be starving. When did you last eat?"

"I ate a bagel and cream cheese on the way to the airport. I'm fine."

"Edgar, let's find a nice restaurant," Marcella said. "He'll be starving before we get back to Morgan Crossroads."

CHAPTER FOURTEEN

FOR THE SECOND TIME THAT DAY, EDGAR WATCHED THE FLIGHT arrivals board. Fred Starnes had been due to arrive just past six o'clock, but a mechanical issue with the airplane had forced him onto a flight that would not arrive until nine o'clock.

Edgar hoped he would recognize Fred, having met him just once, at the closing when he bought the house from Fred. Marcella first suggested that he could hold a sign, such as a limousine driver might. But they hoped to make Fred feel welcome and such a sign might make him feel more like a total stranger.

The plane had only a few passengers, which made the task of picking Fred out of the crowd much easier. Edgar greeted him and helped him carry his luggage to the car.

For several minutes the two men rode in silence. Fred watched tail lights zip around them. Edgar tried to watch Fred.

"We're glad to have you," Edgar said. "Marcella and I have been looking forward to your visit."

An awkward minute or two passed before Fred replied.

"Did you know that I have never been invited to spend time in another person's home?"

"I wasn't aware of that."

"You aren't from Morgan Crossroads, if I remember correctly," Fred said in a hushed voice.

"No, I had never been there until a few days before I bought your house," Edgar said. *Where is this going?*

Fred Starnes stopped following the passing cars and stared forward. "Your wife is the red-haired woman who had been an educator, isn't she?"

"Yes, sir, she is. She taught for several decades."

"Did you know that she was the only person in that community who ever initiated a conversation with me?"

Edgar felt a pounding in his chest as he strained to hear. *What do I say to that?*

"I remember the conversation vividly. I had planted some impatiens in beds on either side of the driveway, and those topiary along the drive that were there when you bought the house."

"Marcella loves beautiful things," Edgar said. "Especially unusual plant life and nice clothes. By the way, the topiary are still there."

"It was just after noon on a Saturday afternoon," Fred said. "I had driven to Haley's Grocery, hoping to find a filet mignon. Your wife took time that day to tell me she thought my plants were gorgeous. That was the word she used. Gorgeous."

"I'm not surprised," Edgar said. "Marcella will be eager to show you what she's done with the back garden."

"I'd love that."

When Edgar and Fred Starnes walked in from the garage, Marcella and Jesse met them.

Marcella held her hand out. Fred took it and bowed slightly.

"We are so excited to have you in our home," she said.

"It was kind of you to invite me."

Jesse introduced himself and shook hands with Fred, whom he towered over.

"I have coffee and dessert. Would anyone like a cup?" Marcella asked.

Edgar and Jesse accepted. Fred asked for water.

"How about a nice little slice of cake?" Marcella asked.

All three men accepted. For the next hour conversation passed around the table, mostly among Edgar, Jesse, and Marcella. Fred spoke only when addressed.

"It's been a long day. Would you mind if I excused myself?" Fred asked.

"Certainly not," Edgar said.

"Let me know if there is anything you need," Marcella said. "There are plenty of fresh linens in your bathroom. There's a tray of fruit and pastries on the table by the window. Jesse poured a fresh pitcher of water just before you and Edgar came in."

"Thank you. That's very kind of you."

"You are so welcome. Mr. Starnes—"

"Call me Fred, please."

"You are so welcome, Fred. Will you be having coffee in the morning?"

"I like fresh orange juice to start my day, but I'll be happy with anything you offer."

"Goodnight, then. We'll see you tomorrow," Marcella said.

"Goodnight," Edgar and Jesse said.

Fred disappeared down the hall to the last door on the right.

"What did Linda Cruz think of your work?" Eva Jo asked her grandson.

"I guess she liked it," Michael said.

"You didn't ask her?"

"No. I figured she would tell me if there was anything wrong."

Let's go at this another way. "What do you think of Linda? She's pretty, you know."

"Of course I know that. Everybody knows that."

"Well?"

"Well what?" Michael asked.

"What do you think of her?"

"Are you trying to hook me up with her?"

Eva Jo stirred buttermilk into her biscuit flour. "Don't you think she's a nice girl?"

"Granny, are you . . ."

"She's been polite every time I've been around her. She dresses nice and–"

"I fixed the awning on her store and she paid me. What else could I expect from her?"

"Nothing. Nothing at all. You worked. She paid. You're even. But wouldn't you like to know her just a little better?"

Michael sipped his coffee, then stirred it even though he'd added nothing to it.

"You're a good-looking young man. She's a good-looking young woman. That's a start, isn't it?"

"Granny, I don't mean any disrespect, but you don't exactly have a stellar record in the relationship department."

Eva Jo pointed her wooden spoon at Michael and with squinted eyes said, "I can't help it if I out-lived one of them.

The other two never stopped fooling around after we got married. So . . ."

"What's in this for you?" Michael asked.

"What's that supposed to mean?"

"I know a little about watching what's going on around me and I could tell something weird was going on around that drug store."

"What's weird about it?" Eva Jo asked as she slid a pan of biscuits into the oven.

"I think you know and Marcella and that nosy one with the little red car."

"Dora Mae?"

"See? I told you. You know exactly what I'm talking about."

"Honey, she's the only nosy one around here with a little red car. We wouldn't need Einstein to help us figure that out."

"Okay, maybe not. But she was circling around that store like she was on patrol."

"When?"

"While I was working on that awning. She thought nobody noticed, I'd bet."

"Maybe she was waiting for a parking place."

Michael cocked one eyebrow and looked out the corner of his eye. "Really? In Morgan Crossroads?"

"Okay, maybe that wasn't what she was doing."

"What was she doing, Granny?"

"Most likely trying to start something. She's been prying around every little nook and cranny of Whipper County for a hundred years or so, however long it's been since she started that dinky paper of hers. My guess is that she's just looking for something to write one of her silly articles about."

"It's more like she was spying on me. I could feel her eyes on me."

"Well, just ignore her. Are you going to do any more work for Linda?"

"I might. She's planning to repaint the inside and she wants to replace the floor tiles."

"There you go. You need to get yourself on over there and put your name in the hat for that job. Get to know her a little better."

Michael threw a sideways glare at his grandmother.

———

When Fred Starnes joined the others for breakfast, Marcella served eggs Benedict, roasted red potatoes, and fresh tomato slices. "I have orange and apple juices, coffee, and milk. Fred, do you still want orange juice?"

She poured orange juice for Jesse and Fred. Jesse poured coffee for Edgar, Marcella, and himself.

"Did you prepare the eggs Benedict?" Fred asked.

"Yes. I hope they're not overcooked," Marcella said.

"They are absolutely delightful. Surely, you couldn't have known they're my favorite breakfast dish."

Marcella felt her cheeks warming. "I'm so glad you enjoyed them."

Fred surveyed Jesse, his eyes scanning the artwork that covered his arms. "What line of work are you in?"

"He's a literature professor," Marcella said, feeling Edgar's knee tapping against hers.

"I teach American Literature at the University of Texas."

"Really," Fred said, his eyes widening. "I was a theater major."

"Where did you study?" Edgar asked.

"Yale. Those were without a doubt some of the best years of my life. Certainly the most hopeful."

"Are you still acting?" Marcella asked.

"Occasionally. I would never declare myself retired for fear that boredom might be my undoing. I'm a choreographer professionally, and I act for pleasure."

"That's wonderful," Marcella said.

Fred smiled for the first time since he'd set foot in Morgan Crossroads. "Pardon me, but I never thought I would meet anyone in this community who appreciated the arts."

"We can be a community of surprises," Marcella said. "There are some wonderful people here, people with hearts of gold."

CHAPTER FIFTEEN

"Put that right over here," Grumpy said, pointing to a spot in the corner of his storage room.

"Give us a hand with it," Ollie said.

Together the men prodded and shoved the antique wardrobe until it fit.

"How are we going to get this thing over to the park for the yard sale?" Grumpy asked.

"Did we decide it was going to be at the park?" Henry asked.

"Where else could it be?" Ollie asked. "Nobody else has room for the hundreds of cars that will be in Morgan Crossroads that day. Speaking of cars, you'd better have your gas tank over at the store full. Those people are going to need gas, too, you know."

"I'm all about thinking positive and all that—when it makes sense, that is. But I wouldn't get my hopes up for a whole gaggle of people to come pouring in here just for a yard sale," Henry said.

Dave Crabtree eased his pickup truck to a stop just

outside the storage room. "Is this where we're supposed to be bringing stuff for the sale?"

"Sure is. Whatcha got?" Ollie asked.

Dave pointed his thumb toward the bed of the truck.

Ollie leaned on the side of the truck and suddenly lost the ability to speak. Hundreds of little heads and houses and animals lined up in dozens of boxes.

Grumpy joined him. "What's this?"

"Yeah, what is all this stuff?" Ollie asked.

Henry peered into the truck's bed. "Those aren't salt and pepper shakers, are they?"

"Yep, that's exactly what they are," Dave said. "I've been trying for twenty years to talk Jewell into getting rid of them. I got them out of the house and I want to keep it that way."

Grumpy lifted one from the boxes. "Milk cows." Then another. "Christmas trees." And another. "Look at this. Out houses. And they've all got holes in the top of them."

"I reckon that's what makes 'em salt shakers," Ollie said. "How many are there?"

Dave hesitated.

"How many of those things have you got here?" Ollie asked.

"Almost twelve hundred pairs."

"Say what?" Henry asked.

"Twelve–" Grumpy started.

"I heard him," Henry said.

"How much are these things worth? A quarter a piece?" Ollie asked.

"If you sell them for that, you'd best not let Jewell know about it. By the way, she said we'd come out better if we sold them a pair at a time."

"That could take years," Ollie said.

"We ain't got but one day for the yard sale, you know."

"Well, here they are," Dave said. "Let's get them unloaded, because I doggone sure ain't hauling them back into that house. Not today. Not ever."

MICHAEL CLOMPER PLACED A BOTTLE OF AFTERSHAVE LOTION, a Butterfinger candy bar, and the latest issue of *People* magazine on the pharmacy checkout counter.

"When did you sneak in?" Linda Cruz asked.

"Just a few minutes ago. You were talking to someone."

Linda ran her fingernail across the scratch and sniff label on the bottle of aftershave lotion and smelled it. "I love the smell of this lotion. It's attractive, but not overpowering."

"It is?" Michael said. "It's the only brand I've ever used, but I've never given it much thought."

"Well, I like it," Linda said as she slid it into a plastic bag. She rang up the candy bar. "My dad used to love Butterfingers. He stopped eating them when he got dentures."

"They'd probably be a little hard to handle," Michael said.

Linda worked the magazine into the bag. "Is there anything else I can get you?"

Michael smiled and turned toward the door. "No, I think this will do it." At the door, he stopped. "There might be one more thing."

"Okay, what would that be?"

He hesitated and surveyed the floor for a second. Then, struggling to make eye contact with her, he said, "I'd like to take you to dinner some time. This evening, if that's not too soon."

Linda took in the question, but couldn't form a reply.

"You don't have to," Michael said. "I mean, if you don't want to, I'd understand." He pulled the door half-way open.

"You have my phone number on file, I think. Just give me a–"

"Okay, I'll take you up on your offer. But I'll be here until six o'clock," Linda said. "Then I'd have to go home and change."

The lump that suddenly appeared in his throat barely outdid the pounding in his chest. "That's okay," Michael said. "We don't have to if you'd rather–"

"Lucy's Cafe doesn't close until nine. If I meet you there at seven, will that be okay?"

"Sure. I'll see you at seven," he said, looking at his watch. *It's almost four o'clock!*

MARCELLA WAS UP EARLY AND BEFORE EDGAR, AS USUAL, making coffee and planning her day. In the darkness outside her kitchen window, mockingbirds tried to out-sing each other.

The shuffle of house slippers on the stone floor announced Jesse's appearance at the kitchen door.

"Good morning," she said.

"You're up early," Jesse said.

"I'm up by this time most mornings. It's quiet and a good time to think about life and all that it brings. How about a cup of coffee and a sweet roll to start your day?"

Marcella poured coffee for Jesse and herself and set a plate of cinnamon rolls she'd bought at the bakery in Porterville on the table.

"How long will you be able to stay with us?"

"My calendar is open for a few weeks, so I can stay for a while if you need me to."

"Your father misses you and your sister. And those grandkids? He really misses the boys running around like little tornadoes. We'd love to have all of you here."

"Gloria wanted to come, but she finishes pastry school in a few weeks and she was afraid she'd miss something important if she came right now. The boys wanted to come with me, but Gloria told them she'd bring them later."

"Oh, Edgar will love hearing that."

"Maybe I can talk her into coming down soon."

"Have you ever considered moving to this area?" Marcella asked.

"I've thought about it, but not seriously. I'm pretty well attached to Texas and I enjoy the Austin area."

"Do you like it here?"

"Don't take me wrong. It's beautiful here and the people are friendly, but there is something special about Austin and that part of Texas is home to me."

"What about your job? Do you enjoy it?"

"There's not another job I'd rather have. I'd love teaching anywhere, but I'm tenured at UT. That would be hard for me to give up."

"Yes, that would be difficult. I'm not sure I could do it if I were ever faced with that choice."

"Don't worry about me. And don't worry about Dad. I can tell by the look in his eye when he's around you that you're all he needs. As long as he has you, he'll be fine," Jesse said.

"Thank you." Marcella held Jesse's hand and smiled. "But always remember that your dad loves you dearly."

Down one hall a shower ran, down the other a door opened.

"Sounds as if we need to get on with cooking breakfast," Jesse said. "What I can do to help?"

LORRAINE HALEY SLID A POUND OF SLICED HAM AND A JAR OF mayonnaise into Polly Brown's bag. "Did you see that man riding in the car with Edgar? I could have sworn he was that Starnes fellow who lived in Marcella's house before her."

"It couldn't have been," Polly said. "He went back to California or somewhere out that way."

"Well, if it wasn't Fred Starnes, the man has a double running around Morgan Crossroads," Lorraine said.

Dora Mae Crawford hoisted a five-pound bag of potatoes onto the checkout stand. "He was quite an odd little duck, don't you think?"

"Oh, I wouldn't say there was anything especially odd about him," Polly said.

"There is, though," Dora Mae said. She stomped her feet into a firm position, squinted, and held one hand in front of her pointing upward like she was counting to one. "If you're walking down the sidewalk and you speak to someone and they just ignore you like you were an old glass doorknob, there is something strange about him."

"Did he do that to you?" Lorraine asked.

"No, but I suspect it's only because I never met him on a sidewalk. If I had, though," Dora Mae said, wagging her bent finger at Lorraine, "that crooked little nose of his would have been pointing across the road, completely ignoring me."

"Where did you come up with an idea like that?" Polly asked.

"I have it on good authority that he's uppity. And that's what uppity people do," Dora Mae said.

"Uppity," Lorraine said. "Somebody told you that Fred Starnes is uppity, and now you don't like him. Have I got that right?"

"I can't divulge my sources, you know."

"How would you define uppity?" Polly asked.

Dora Mae said, "Everybody knows what uppity is."

"Maybe I've got it all wrong," Lorraine said.

"Okay, I'll tell you what uppity is. Uppity is when they think they're up here." Dora Mae held her hand as far above her head as she could. "And you're way down here somewhere," she said, holding her finger tips at her knees.

"Dora Mae, why do you think Fred Starnes is uppity?"

"Oh, you people," she said, her words more drawn out than usual. "I witnessed it with my own eyes and ears. That's all I can say."

Eva Jo walked in the front door and joined Polly and Dora Mae at the checkout lane. "What's all you can say?" she asked, elbowing Polly. "Did I miss out on something juicy?"

"I was standing at the window at the Dairy Bar waiting on my extra thick banana malt when Fred Starnes climbed his little self out of whatever kind of car that was and stomped up there right beside me."

"Fred Starnes isn't big enough to do much stomping," Eva Jo said.

Lorraine and Polly laughed.

Dora Mae drew in a deep breath and blew it out. "Well, he did. And you know what he told that poor kid behind the window? He slid his burger back through the window like it was a hockey puck and told him it was the greasiest double cheeseburger he'd ever seen. I didn't see a thing wrong with it. I'm telling you, it looked just like one I might cook."

"Dora Mae, Honey, that's not being uppity," Polly said.

"Sure isn't," Eva Jo said. "That's just indigestion talking."

"I LIKE THAT LOOK," LINDA CRUZ SAID.

"I didn't know I had a look," Michael said, his eyes scanning his blue and black plaid shirt and blue jeans.

"It's kind of rustic, but not exactly."

Michael shrugged. "It's just me, whatever that is."

At the last remaining table in Lucy's Cafe, Michael offered Linda her choice of seats, then sat across from her.

Stella brought menus and water. "Well, it's a pleasant surprise to see you two in here this evening." She gave Michael one of those I know what you're up to looks wrapped in a smile. "The special tonight is pork chops. If you don't like that, the meat loaf is real good."

Linda and Michael placed their orders. Michael took a sip of his sweet tea. Linda asked for unsweetened, then stirred artificial sweetener into it. They both held their glasses in a vise-like grip, as if letting go might unleash something else, something like the ability to speak.

"How," they both said.

"You first," Michael said.

"No, you first," Linda said. "How was your day?"

Boring as usual, he wanted to say. "Not bad. Helped my grandmother clean up the barn. And I washed my truck."

"I didn't know you had a truck. Last I knew, you were driving Eva Jo's."

"You mean, what's left of it. I had a truck before I shipped out to the Middle East. When I got back, it wouldn't start and I couldn't figure out why, so it's been in Grumpy's shop for a while."

"I presume he fixed it," Linda said.

"Runs like a new one now. I still have some other work to do on it. So how was your day?"

"Typical, I guess. Filled prescriptions and sold a little of everything from bandages to fingernail polish."

"Let's see," Stella said, surveying the table for an open

spot large enough for a dinner plate. "Linda, you had the meatloaf with mashed potatoes and carrots. Michael, yours was the fried shrimp with sweet potato fries and a side salad."

"It looks great," Michael said.

"Good. I'll be right back to top off your tea glasses," Stella said.

Michael and Linda ate their meals, which they followed with coconut cake and coffee.

"I'm glad we did this," Linda said.

"I am, too. I was afraid you might say no."

"Why would you think that?"

"I don't know. I thought you might have somebody somewhere else that you were involved with. Or maybe you were too busy."

"Well, to set your mind at ease, there is no somebody somewhere else. How about you?" Linda asked.

"Social life and I seem to go in opposite directions," Michael said. "This is Morgan Crossroads, you know."

"Yes, it is. But that can be nice, you know. When I lived in the city, life just seemed too busy to be sociable. There was always something to do or somewhere to go. One friend would tug at me from one side and another would beg me to go do something different with her."

"Boring can be nice," Michael said. His hand flew up as if to stop his words from traveling any further. "I mean boring towns. You're not boring. Not at all. I mean . . ."

Linda smiled. "I know what you mean. I like to think of Morgan Crossroads as sleepy, not boring."

"It's sleepy, alright. Most of the time it's so fast asleep that I think I can hear it snoring. But then I figure out it's just Granny snoring.

Linda laughed. "I'm going to tell her what you said."

"Go ahead. She knows she sounds like a freight train when she sleeps."

They sipped their coffee and took refills when Stella offered.

"So, what is your social life like?" Michael asked.

"Nearly nonexistent," Linda said. "My social interaction is more or less limited to the customers I see through the course of a day. I love helping my customers, but sometimes it feels odd that I know more about their medical history than I do about their children or their grandkids. Would you believe that I don't know where ninety percent of my customers live, even though Morgan Crossroads barely shows up on the state map?"

Michael leaned in. "Don't feel bad about that. I only know where everybody lives because this is where I grew up. It's kinda like you're born with it around here."

"Do you know where I live?" Linda asked.

Michael stopped to think. "You know, I can't say I do. I've never thought about it." *It's a good thing I didn't offer to pick her up.*

"You'd be forgiven for not knowing," Linda said. "I live in Porterville, the last street before the city limit sign going west out of town."

Stella left the checks on the table and offered more coffee. Michael and Linda both refused.

Michael reached for Linda's check, but missed when she snatched it away.

"Let me buy your dinner," Michael said.

"Thank you. I'll pay for mine," Linda said. "Maybe next time."

CHAPTER SIXTEEN

IVY LEAVES MOVED IN THE BREEZE, PRODUCING A LIGHT rustling chorus that answered the stronger calls of the maples and sycamores beyond the shade of the pergola.

"I love what you've done with this garden," Fred Starnes said. "There's a peacefulness here that I've rarely experienced."

"This area was Marcella's idea," Edgar said.

"I wanted a protected place where I could relax and enjoy solitude, somewhere to come at night and listen to nature and see the billions of stars out there." Marcella said. She pointed across the garden. "We planted those decorative grasses over there just so they would move in the breeze that comes around that corner of the house."

Fred fixed his eyes on the tall grasses as if he were looking into their center, into a place no one else could see. "There is something graceful and quite musical about them, a ballet that no human could choreograph, the swaying and the whispering notes that none of us could compose."

Marcella glanced at Edgar who was, as she had been,

watching Fred. She wondered if Edgar was as curious as she about what Fred was thinking.

"Mister Starnes, Fred," Marcella said. "Were you ever a dancer?"

Fred stiffened, if only for a moment. "No. I'm a choreographer." He spoke with his back still toward Marcella and Edgar.

Edgar locked eyes with Marcella. "Did you ever have aspirations of dancing professionally?" Edgar asked.

Fred's eyes focused on the stone pavement between his feet. "Why do you ask?" His tone was so soft that it was barely audible.

Marcella swallowed and stole a questioning glance toward Edgar. "Fred, we found something . . ." *Should I say this?* She forced the lump in her throat away. "We found something very personal that we think might have belonged to you."

Fred turned slowly. *The letter.* There it was in Edgar's hand. Yellowed and brittle. Fragile and beaten, yet so powerful that it could force back to life memories which had long since been put to rest. He took the letter from Edgar and held it on open palms. One tear fell on the envelope and then another, each expanding into a ring that looked as old as the paper itself.

Marcella gripped Edgar's hand and fought back her own tears.

Edgar dropped his gaze to the ground and closed his eyes.

OLLIE SMITH SET HIS RC COLA ON THE FLOOR OF THE general store porch and bit a chunk out of a chocolate Moon

Pie. "It seems we have a minor problem," he said, chewing as he spoke.

"What might that be?" Henry Brown asked.

"There's one little detail that we never did come up with any kind of agreement on," Ollie said.

"I know you're not bringing up the fried pickle idea again," Grumpy said.

"That wasn't my idea. It was what's his name's..." Ollie snapped his fingers three or four times. "Johnny Mack Durant. I can't stand fried pickles so you won't have to worry about me voting for them."

"Okay, we never talked about who would count the money," Henry said.

"I didn't figure we had to talk about that," Ollie said. "As good as you are at counting money and stashing it in those old coffee cans. Surely you can–"

"Oh, I can count it alright, but somebody's got to collect it when all those people buy stuff. A nickel here and a dollar there will add up if you do it enough times, but there needs to be more than one person doing it."

"Okay, you probably won't be there to collect anything anyway," Ollie said.

"Surely you'll have this place open, won't you? Remember, some of those folks are going to be needing gas for the ride back home. Or maybe one of them Moon Pies or RC Colas," Grumpy said, nodding toward Ollie's snack.

"Well, we've gone and got ourselves off track now," Ollie said. "We can figure out how to do the money part of it. The big problem is this. That country singer we were paying to come run through a few songs says he can't make it now. Something came up, he said."

"I can guess what came up," Henry said. "He decided he

wasn't going to drive all the way up here from Birmingham for fifty dollars. I bet that's what came up."

"Whatever the reason was, we're in a mess right now. We've got ourselves a shindig coming up and nobody to do the entertaining."

"We could get Cecil up there and do some of his hog calling," Grumpy said.

"That ain't hog calling," Ollie said.

"That's his choir voice," Henry said, laughing. "I've heard him calling hogs and I can tell you I'd a lot rather listen to him doing that."

"Seriously, fellows, we've got a big hole in the day that we've got to fill some way. We can't expect people to drive all the way up in this valley and not give them any kind of entertainment."

"Okay, so who knows somebody that can come on short notice? You know we don't have but a couple of months to pull this off," Henry said.

"It's two weeks, not two months," Ollie said.

"That's not what the flyers you put out said," Grumpy said.

"Why, it is, too. The first day of July is what I told them to put on it."

Grumpy scratched his head. "Weren't you the one that tacked 'em up on all them telephone poles?"

"I sure was. Thought I was going to wear out my arm driving all those tacks."

"Well, you might want to look at them again," Henry said. He pointed at a bright yellow paper on the utility pole across the parking lot. "That one over there says the first day of September."

"Aw, foot. Who did that?" Ollie asked.

"I don't know, but I think we ought to go by that so we

don't start confusing people," Henry said. "We've waited all these years to fix up that park. Surely to Pete we can wait another couple of months."

Grumpy stepped halfway into the front door of the store and stopped. "Somebody better dig up another singer or a Houdini or something between now and then. Ain't but one person around here that calls himself a professional musician, and that's Charlie Waterton."

"From what I hear, he's like a one man demolition team whenever he sits down at a piano," Ollie said. "My wife saw him at the homecoming at the Third Pentecostal Holiness Revival Church down in the valley two or three years ago. Said he shook a vase of flowers plumb off the top of a piano."

"I was there that day. The way he was flailing himself around on that piano bench, you'd have thought Liberace had come back around," Grumpy said. "I thought he was going to jump out of his skin when that vase hit the floor."

"We'll come up with somebody to do the entertaining," Henry said.

STILL LOOKING DOWN AT THE LETTER, FRED ASKED, "WHERE did you get this?"

"We had some repairs made in the kitchen. The workers found it inside the wall," Edgar said.

"This was never to be seen again." Fred lifted his head and focused his attention somewhere beyond the yard. "Not ever."

"Josephine Starnes sounds like a wonderful lady. Was she your grandmother?" Marcella asked.

Fred nodded.

"How well did you know her?"

Fred turned to face Edgar and Marcella. "I knew her very well."

"We assume your father was Frederick Starnes and you are Frederick Starnes, Junior," Edgar said.

"I am Frederick, Junior. Fred to most people, though."

"Tell us about your grandmother," Marcella said. "I'd love to know about her."

"Grandmother was beautiful, like a petite piece of fine art. She was strong and frail at the same time. Poor health drew limits on her physical capabilities, but in a battle of wits she would cower to no one if she believed she was right."

"In the letter she sounded like an iron-willed woman," Edgar said.

"That, she was. But the thing I remember most was her kind spirit. Her demeanor was gentle like a breeze. She was my most loyal supporter from the day I was born until she passed on. As a youngster, I spent every summer in Connecticut with her. She and I would steal away, as she called it, and go into the city—that's what she called New York City. We would attend performances of the Metropolitan Opera and sometimes, we would spend an entire day there, taking in theater and opera on the same day. She would take me to the finest hotels for lunch."

"That sounds like such fun," Marcella said. "I love theater and although I've never been to a live opera performance, I've enjoyed listening to several. Did you study dance formally?"

"Yes. I started very young. I don't think my grandfather ever knew that Grandmother paid for my dance training. He would have been livid, had he known. Absolutely livid."

"I understood you to say you don't dance," Marcella said.

"Actually, I believe I said that I'm a choreographer. I saw Nureyev once in Paris and thought I'd gone to heaven, sitting there completely absorbed in a performance by one of my heroes. I came back to America with my heart set upon the idea that I could be an American Nureyev."

"What happened to that idea?" Marcella asked.

Fred lifted the letter from his lap. "This happened."

No one spoke for several seconds. Edgar surveyed his shoe laces. Fred stared across the lawn into the trees. Marcella attempted to read Fred's face, searching for more.

"My father disapproved of me in ways that I can't explain. From the day I was born, he somehow decided that I would be an outsider to him. And I always was. Oh, he paid for boarding school and college, but only for those parts he felt obliged to pay. My mother ran off to Europe as soon as she got over the childbirth. That's how my grandmother came to be my loyalest supporter."

"In the letter, we read that your father was ordered not to pass along your grandfather's inheritance," Edgar said.

"It wouldn't have mattered. He never intended to pass anything on to me, or at least, that's what I believe."

"You told us the letter stopped you becoming a dancer," Marcella said. "How so?"

"All of my life I hoped my grandfather or my father—any man in my family, for that matter—would welcome me into their lives. That letter represented the lock on the door that closed me off from that possibility forever. From there, life went downhill. For a long time, it did."

CHAPTER SEVENTEEN

"How do you know Linda doesn't like you?" Eva Jo asked while she frosted a fresh carrot cake.

"She wouldn't let me buy her dinner," Michael said.

"What else?"

"Nothing else. That's it. I tried to pick up the tab for both of us and she let me know right quick that she would pay for her own."

"Good," Eva Jo said. "That just means she can take care of herself and she won't need you trailing along behind her mopping up." She set the empty frosting bowl and a spoon in front of Michael. "Did she enjoy herself?"

Michael scraped the remaining frosting from the sides of the bowl. "I thought she was having a good time. But now, I think maybe she was just being nice."

"Baloney. You just need to ask her out again. And don't wait around forever. Somebody else might beat you to her."

"She's not a contest prize, Granny." He licked the last speck of frosting from the spoon. "Have you and your gossip buddies got something sneaky going on?"

"Where did you get the idea that I have any gossip buddies?"

Michael cocked his head and looked at his grandmother through squinted eyes.

"And who said anything about a contest?"

"Nobody in particular, but you sure act like you're trying to win one."

"Nobody said anything about that. I just think Linda Cruz would make a fine companion for some lucky young man."

"Do you remember the time you told me we weren't going to have any more hard rock music on the radio because it took up too much room in the air?"

"Michael, you were ten or twelve years old. How did you remember that?"

"I was just thinking about when you used to be a lot better at lying."

POLLY TURNED OFF STELLA'S HAIR DRYER. "DID I HEAR something about Eva Jo's grandson dating Linda Cruz?"

Dora Mae dropped her soap opera magazine on the floor.

Lorraine Haley stopped her conversation with Jewell Crabtree.

"Who told you that?" Stella asked.

"Oh, I don't remember. My washing machine quit the other day, so I had to take a load of towels over to Lassiter's Laundromat. Somebody in there was talking about it," Polly said.

"When did they start dating?" Dora Mae asked.

"I don't know that they were dating," Stella said.

"Whoever I heard talking about it said he saw them having dinner together," Polly said.

"Is that true, Stella?" Dora Mae asked as she clawed through her purse for an ink pen.

"Oh, I wouldn't know about that. People come in everyday and have dinner with someone they're not dating or married to."

"But this is Linda Cruz we're talking about," Jewell said.

Dora Mae jumped up and headed toward the door. "I'm going over and ask Linda. I'll get the straight answer. News like this doesn't happen every day."

Polly stopped Dora just before she closed the door behind herself. "Honey, don't you think we should take those rollers down first?"

"PERHAPS WE CAN MOVE INTO THE KITCHEN OR THE DEN," Marcella said.

"Let's do," Edgar said.

"Would you men like a cup of coffee or a glass of iced tea?"

"I'd like coffee, please. No sugar or cream," Fred said.

"If you don't mind my asking, how did that letter come to be inside the kitchen wall?" Edgar asked.

Marcella served iced tea for Edgar and black coffee for Fred. "I'd love to know how you learned about Morgan Crossroads. My mind has been busy ever since the repairmen found the letter. And I've been trying to imagine how a man in Hollywood might hear of this place then build such a fine home here," Marcella said.

Fred held his coffee cup with both hands and stared for a long moment into its contents. He inhaled, then exhaled slowly through inflated cheeks. "Does the Greendyke name mean anything to either of you?"

"Yes, I remember that the Greendyke family owned this land before you, but they lived out of state. I can't say that I ever met any of them," Marcella said. "How did you come to know them?"

"George Greendyke, whose grandchildren sold this land to me, was Grandmother Starnes's oldest brother. My understanding is that he would take the train from his home in Chicago to Chattanooga. There is no sign of it now, but he had a primitive cabin built near that line of trees that borders the rear of the property. Coming here was his way of finding solitude, according to Grandmother. She called it getting away from the rattle and business of city life."

"Had you been here prior to buying the property?" Edgar asked.

"Once, when I was very young. I came one summer with him and two of his grandchildren. I had never experienced anything like it. Everything around me seemed so primitive. There were no tall buildings and the sidewalks seemed so empty. I don't recall the name or the route we took to get there, but we went swimming in a narrow river somewhere up in the northern end of the valley. I remember turning off the road and driving on a dirt path across a field to it. There was a deer standing beside a tree. It ran off and we hung our clothes there. It was the first live deer I'd ever seen. I loved that experience, but hated going with Uncle George to fish. Such drudgery, it seemed to me."

"So you built your own getaway here," Marcella said.

"Yes, ma'am. In some odd way, I thought it might feel the same to me as I had remembered."

"Did it?" Edgar asked.

"Not for a moment."

"What was different?" Marcella asked.

"Everything. Or perhaps nothing. Please forgive me if I

say something offensive, but there was nothing familiar here. There were no news stands or taverns. In the city, and in Los Angeles, life carries with it a cacophony of sounds. There are car horns blasting away, trains rattling by, and people brushing past each other without a thought. I found it terribly difficult to connect with people in any meaningful way here. It seems life goes by without making a sound here. If I asked the grocer for filet mignon, she looked at me as though I had requested escargot.

"Lorraine Haley," Edgar said. "She's actually quite a friendly lady. If you'd asked for a T-bone, I bet she'd have offered you the finest she had."

"Did you ever spend time with any of the men?" Marcella asked.

Fred straightened himself in his chair and swatted the air. "I tried a time or two, but I found it hard to...how should I say it? I found it hard to join in their conversations. I stopped for gas at Brown's General Store one time just after I arrived in the area. There were men rocking in the porch chairs, talking about farming and hunting and working on cars—all things that I know nothing about. They looked at me as if I had landed a Lear jet in front of the store."

"Maybe they were just impressed with your car. What were you driving?" Edgar asked.

"A Bentley. I'd had it for several years, so it was far from new."

"I doubt very seriously any of them had ever seen a Bentley automobile in person," Marcella said. "In fact, I'm not so sure that I have."

"Would you believe that the owner would not take my credit card for gasoline?"

Marcella and Edgar chuckled.

"That's Henry. If he had his way there wouldn't be a

banking industry. He doesn't trust them," Marcella said. "If it weren't for coffee cans I don't know where he would store his money."

"He wouldn't take my credit card either," Edgar said. "So don't feel bad about that."

"Actually, there is a sound to life around here," Marcella said. "But it's different. You're more likely to hear a tractor rattling by with a hay wagon or women laughing about something than you are to hear a train."

"If you hoped for someone to brush past you on the sidewalk, you'd probably have to cross the street so that there'd be two people there at the same time," Edgar said, chuckling.

"You might find it hard to fit in at first, but I'm sure Morgan Crossroads would grow on you if you gave it another chance," Marcella said.

"Oh, I don't think I could do that. Mrs. Garrison, I know that you and your husband appreciate the arts, but you are the only ones that I can possibly imagine doing so. That leaves me in a very lonely place. Art runs through my veins. I survive on being able to write and produce art for the theater. I no longer dance, but it brings me more joy than I can express when I have the opportunity to help another person express him or herself through dance or theatrical performance. Where would I ever be able to do that in this community?"

"These people might surprise you," Marcella said.

CHAPTER EIGHTEEN

FRED STARNES RODE TO HUNTSVILLE WITH JESSE TO PICK UP A suit that Edgar had left with the tailor.

Marcella and Edgar sat on the bench in the garden and took in the fresh morning air.

"Did you enjoy yourself out at Ollie's farm yesterday?" Marcella asked.

"Yes, I did. I don't remember ever being on a farm other than Eva Jo's. You wouldn't believe the things that have been collected and stored in his barn for the fundraiser sale."

"I'll be excited to see what all they have," Marcella said.

"There's more than what's in that barn. Ollie and Grumpy are worried we might not sell it all."

"Is everything else coming together?"

"They, or rather we, have lost our entertainment for the day. Without that, they're worried we might not draw a crowd large enough to buy everything."

"Who did you have lined up for the entertainment?" Marcella asked.

"I have no idea what his name was, but I understand he

was a country singer from Birmingham. He canceled less than a week after he agreed to come. I wish I could come up with some ideas to help them out, but I have so very little experience with this kind of thing. I'd wouldn't know where to start," Edgar said.

"Are the men insisting on a singer, or would some other form of entertainment do?"

"Right now I think they would take an organ grinder and a monkey if they found one that would accept the invitation."

LINDA CRUZ HAD JUST HUNG A SIGN ANNOUNCING A CLOSE out sale on greeting cards. When she stepped down from the stool, a familiar drawl sounded.

"That side is a tad too high," Dora Mae said, pointing to the right.

"I didn't hear you come in," Linda said.

Dora Mae held her hand out, palm up. "That's because the clapper fell out of your door bell. Here, you might need this."

Linda took the clapper from Dora Mae. "Thanks."

"The right side. It's too high," Dora Mae said as she studied the sale sign. "Did you ever replace your refrigerator?"

Linda climbed onto the step stool. "How's that?"

"Too low. You know you could probably have that little fridge repaired."

"That's close enough," Linda said after she adjusted the sign. "No one will notice if it's a little bit off."

"Todd Jenkins stopped in a few days ago."

"Did he?" Dora Mae feigned innocence.

"You don't remember him?"

"Of course I remember him. He won the spelling bee four consecutive times if I remember correctly. I'd have to check to be sure. And let's see what else. He made more A's in algebra than anyone else in his grade. I'm sure my niece would have had more if she'd had any interest in algebra," Dora Mae said.

"My uncle was very fond of Todd. I never asked him, but I wouldn't be surprised if he memorized every accomplishment that Todd ever had."

"Did he repair the fridge?"

"No. I bought a new one from the hardware store in Porterville."

Dora Mae's shoulders fell. "Todd couldn't fix the old one?"

"He might have been able to. I never asked him."

THERE WAS A GOOD TURNOUT FOR THE REGULAR TUESDAY morning Rosebud Circle meeting. Linda was there, wedged into her place at the table between Jewell Crabtree and Dora Mae. Dora Mae and the Pearle twins talked over each other, vying across the table for Linda's attention.

Eva Jo brought a pan of sticky cinnamon rolls she'd made from scratch. Lorraine Haley eyed them and argued with herself for ten minutes before she softened enough to reach for one.

Stella served a fancy new coffee blend the grocery salesman had talked her into trying. "If your ladies don't love it, I'll buy it back," he'd said.

Marcella finished her toast and eggs, then stood and tried to get their attention. Try as she might, there was no chance of breaking into Dora Mae's contest with the Pearle twins until Eva Jo let out an ear-piercing whistle that she'd learned from her brother sixty years earlier.

"Thank you," Marcella said to Eve Jo. "Before we get into our normal discussion, I just learned this morning that Doctor Sue's mother passed away last night. We need to send flowers and find out where to take food."

"I'll see to that," Gertrude Gleaves said.

"Okay. We should all call to check in on her, too. Does anyone have anything else that we should talk about?" Marcella asked.

"What about this fund raiser the men are trying to get together?" Polly Brown asked. "Henry says they're trying to raise enough money to get the park cleaned up."

"I know they're collecting everything they can get their hands on for a yard sale," Jewell said.

"According to Ollie Smith, it will be the biggest sale ever for this part of the state," Gertrude said. "He came out to the house last week and loaded his truck with stuff."

"Henry says they've got a minor issue with the entertainment," Polly said.

"What entertainment? Why would they want entertainment at a yard sale?" Dora Mae asked.

"I haven't been able to get a logical answer to that one yet," Polly said. "But they've also got it in their minds that we're going to come up with all kinds of cakes and pies for them to sell."

"Grumpy and Ollie talked to me about ordering enough ground beef and hamburger buns to feed a small army," Lorraine said.

"So, what's the deal with the entertainment?" Dora Mae asked.

"They see this fund raiser as an all-day event with all kinds of food and games and live entertainment wrapped around that yard sale," Polly said. "They had some part-time country singer from Birmingham lined up, but he had to cancel."

"What do they want us to do about it?" Eva Jo said. "I can't think of anybody around here that could entertain a crowd for more than about thirty seconds."

"Henry didn't ask for suggestions, but they're running out of time and I thought maybe we could come up with an idea or two," Polly said.

"Okay, let's make this our project for this month," Marcella said. "I'll talk to Edgar. Maybe we can help them."

"I don't know," Jewell said. "The men around here are about as prideful–"

"You mean knot-headed," Eva Jo said.

Jewell laughed. "I was trying to be nice. These men don't like to be outdone, especially by women."

"We'll just have to be creative with our suggestions," Marcella said.

"I'm pretty sure the guys are thinking about some kind of singer," Gertrude said. "And to most of them there are only two kinds of singing—country and gospel."

"Let's give it a few days. I have an idea that I can look into," Marcella said. "If anyone else comes up with anything, call me and I'll pass it along to Edgar."

"Henry's trying to act like it doesn't much matter to him what they do, but I can tell you he thinks they're going to flop if they don't come up with something pretty soon."

"I could write an article about it," Dora Mae said. She made an arc in the air, outlining the headline. "Men desperate for help. Fundraiser about to flop."

"I'm not so sure I'd try that if I were you," Eva Jo said. "That is, unless you want to get run out of town for the rest of your life."

The Pearle twins snickered.

Linda watched and listened, bemused.

After confirming there were no other matters to discuss, Marcella announced, "This meeting of the Rosebud Circle is adjourned."

"I wish you'd look at this," Grumpy said.

Edgar looked up, down, and around the barn and everywhere he looked there was another stack of boxes or pile of furniture. "Quite impressive."

"I don't know if we should be impressed or worried," said Ollie, remembering how much was stored in his own barn.

"Why would you be worried?" Edgar asked.

"Worried we'll have to do something with this stuff if we don't get rid of it at the yard sale," Grumpy said. "And this ain't all of it. My storage building at the shop is plumb full, too. Can't hold another stick."

"Well, I'd say we need to be very creative if we're to draw enough people to sell everything," Edgar said. He had followed Ollie out to Grumpy's farm after a drawn out discussion on the front porch at Brown's General Store had failed to yield any satisfactory solutions.

"It was enough work creating room to hold this stuff," Ollie said. "I swear for the life of me I can't imagine us ever selling this much stuff. Shoot, I never knew there was this much stuff in Morgan Crossroads. Where'd it all come from?"

Edgar looked over the furniture thoroughly enough to

recognize that some pieces were antique and valuable. "I have an idea. Give me a day or two to check into some things and I'll get back to you."

"Take as long as you need, I mean so long as it don't take you past yard sale day."

CHAPTER NINETEEN

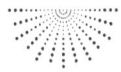

"Come on in," Eva Jo shouted from the kitchen.

"I can't. The screen door's locked," Marcella shouted.

"It's not locked. Just yank on it."

Marcella gave the screen door an extra hard tug and made her way through the living room and dining room into the kitchen.

"Do I have flour on the top of my head?" Eva Jo asked, bowing her head low so Marcella could see.

"No, not yet," Marcella said. "What happened?"

"Oh, you wouldn't believe it if I told you. I stuck the mixer in that bowl over there and when I turned it on, the thing flew into a rage and slung flour everywhere. Look at this mess."

"What are you trying to make?"

"It's Michael's birthday, so I thought I'd whip up a mayonnaise cake for him."

"Excuse me," Marcella said as if questioning Eva Jo.

"Mayonnaise cake. You've eaten it yourself a dozen times and just didn't know it." Eva Jo sat the mixing bowl in front of Marcella. "Here. You can lick the bowl."

Marcella looked at the bowl as if it might be evidence at a crime scene.

"Go ahead. It's not going to bite you," Eva Jo said. "I promise you won't keel over from it."

Marcella ran a finger along the edge of the ceramic bowl and touched it to her tongue. A slight smile crept across her face as she went for a longer swipe.

"I told you," Eva Jo said. "What does it taste like?"

"Chocolate cake—a rich chocolate."

"Yep. And if Michael saves you a slice, you'll find out how moist it is."

Eva Jo handed Marcella a small rubber spatula. "Here. This will work better than your finger."

Marcella savored the last morsel from the bowl's edge, then pushed it aside. "Have you heard anything about that fundraiser the men are putting together?"

"Oh, Lord. Every time I'm in Haley's somebody starts in talking about that yard sale. Talk is, they've collected enough junk to cover that park they're trying to fix up. Why?"

"I understand they've run into a little problem finding somebody to provide the entertainment," Marcella said.

"I heard something about that, but to be honest with you, I don't see why they think they need to entertain people, anyway." Eva Jo poured coffee for Marcella and herself. "Here, you can wash that cake down. If anybody shows up for the sale, they'll be here to see how much stuff they can get for nothing. Seems to me that'd be entertainment enough. I can't see them driving all the way up in this valley just to watch somebody get up and prove how bad a singer they are."

"But what if the men were to find another form of entertainment? Something that had never been done in this area. What then?" Marcella asked.

"I can tell by the way your forehead's wrinkling that you've got something stirring up there. What have you come up with now? Wait." Eva Jo straightened herself in the chair and planted her arms on the table. "Maybe I need to prop up for this one."

"It's not that bad, Eva Jo. Can you keep this idea between the two of us?"

"Probably. Depends what it is."

"I think we should ask Fred Starnes to put on a performance of some kind—maybe a stage play or something like that."

"Fred Starnes? Honey, you might have to keep that one between you and yourself and leave me out of it. What in the world could somebody like him, somebody so high falootin–what could he possibly put on that people around here might actually enjoy?"

Marcella pulled closer to the table. "He's a professional choreographer. He's written and produced stage performances."

"I don't know quite what a choreographer is," Eva Jo said. "But what has him writing and producing stage shows got to do with a yard sale in Morgan Crossroads, Alabama? Maybe if he can sing a little Conway Twitty or Buddy Holly or even a Smokey Robinson tune or two I could see it. Or even some gospel music. But I just don't know about any of that other stuff."

"I'd like to ask him to produce one of his works and use people from the local area to play the parts. I'm sure we could use the church hall for it. I'd love to see him work. I bet he can draw talents out of people that they don't even know they have."

"I don't know, Honey. That's way over my head. I know there's not a single acting bone in my body. Not one. Now I can sew and I'm pretty good with a hammer and a saw if he needed somebody like that. And I'm a pretty decent cook, except when my mixer goes haywire. But the acting and singing part? That's going to have to be somebody else's job."

Marcella hugged herself. "I'm so excited. Look at these goose bumps."

———

"I GIVE UP," DORA MAE CRAWFORD SAID.

"Give up on what?" Polly asked.

"Don't tell me you're giving up life as a reporter," Jewell Crabtree said.

"No, I couldn't do that. People in this valley depend on me to keep them up to date with all the goings on."

"Then what else could you be giving up on?" Lorraine Haley asked.

"I give up on this idea of finding Linda Cruz a man. I just give up."

"That doesn't sound like you," Polly said as she rinsed Dora Mae's hair.

"It's a lost cause. I've come to the unfortunate conclusion that Linda has no interest in men," Dora Mae said.

"Where on God's green earth did you ever come up with an idea like that?" Jewell asked.

"I used my very best persuasive abilities—you know, the kind that only the best reporters have—to arrange for a young man to meet up with her. And do you want to know what happened?"

Before anyone could answer no, Dora Mae said, "Not a thing. It was as if one of Santa's elves had visited her."

Polly laughed. Jewell shook her head. The Pearle twins looked at each other, bemused.

"What was she supposed to do, go nuts like Willie Nelson had visited her?" Polly asked.

"She could've at least shown an interest in him. But from what I gather, she just treated him like any other customer."

"Well, at least we know your mystery guy was treated kindly," Jewell said.

One of the Pearle twins asked, "Dora Mae, did you ever ask this young man if he was in the market for a lady to share his life?"

"Not exactly, but—and I don't mean to be offensive— what would either of you know about attracting men? You are sixty-something years old and as far as I know, neither of you has ever been on a single date."

"Be nice, Dora Mae," Polly said. "You might want to look in the mirror before you spout off too much."

"Okay, I'm sorry ladies. That might not have been an appropriate response," Dora Mae said.

"Did you ask him?" the other twin asked.

"Not exactly. But he did seem excited when I told him that Linda had a refrigerator that was on the blink."

"Did Todd get the job?" Polly asked.

"No. And who says we're talking about Todd Jenkins?"

"You. You as much as spilled the beans on yourself last time you were in here," Polly said.

"Did it ever occur to you that Linda has a mind of her own?" Jewell asked. "She might have somebody cornered somewhere that none of us knows about."

"Well, I'm watching Michael Clomper," Polly said. "I wouldn't be at all surprised if Eva Jo sends him back over there to ask her out to dinner again."

Dora Mae settled into a pout and stayed there while Polly and Jewell discussed a new potato casserole recipe.

CHAPTER TWENTY

A<small>FTER HE AND</small> M<small>ARCELLA CLEARED THE DINNER DISHES FROM</small> the table, Jesse offered to clean the kitchen.

Marcella, Edgar, and Fred Starnes retired to the den with coffee.

"Marcella has a request for you," Edgar said.

"Sure. How can I help you?" Fred asked.

"The men in Morgan Crossroads are planning a fundraiser to help cover the cost of renovating our local park. They desperately need someone who can provide professional entertainment for the people who come to town that day."

"How much have they budgeted for entertainment?" Fred asked.

"Oh, that's not the issue," Marcella said. "They someone lined up, but he's backed out now."

"We need someone who can arrange the entertainment for us," Edgar said.

"I don't think I could do that," Fred said. "I assume it was a country singer who canceled." He held his hand up as if to hold back comments. "I say that only because I remember how people here enjoy country music. I wouldn't know one country artist from another. I'm afraid I'd be no good for that job."

"We're thinking about a different type of entertainment than anyone has ever seen in Morgan Crossroads," Marcella said.

"And what role do you see me playing in this?" Fred asked.

Marcella cleared her throat. "We'd like you to produce a piece of your work and have the performance the day of the fundraiser." *There, I said it.*

"Mrs. Garrison, Marcella, do you realize what a huge undertaking you're asking of me?"

"Probably not. But I can imagine it will be a challenge."

"And I can promise you'll have all the help the people of this community can manage," Edgar said.

Fred pushed his chair back and looked toward the crown molding above Marcella. A full minute of silence passed. "How can you be sure this community will welcome any production that I might direct?"

Marcella clasped her hands in front of her and leaned toward Fred. "You have my word. I know these people and I'm sure that in the beginning, some of them will balk and grumble. But I also know that when it's over, they'll be among the proudest people you've ever met."

"Fred, these people don't dislike you," Edgar said. "What you interpret as hatred or silence is nothing more than one stranger looking at another. None of them knows you well enough to dislike you."

"I'm just not sure about this," Fred said.

"If you think I'm stepping out of bounds here, feel free to tell me," Marcella said. "But I remember so vividly the feeling I had the first time I read your grandmother's letter. I could vicariously feel the love she had for you and the joy that you and your work brought her."

"She did love me," Fred said. "I grew up believing she was the only person on this planet who truly loved me for who I was."

"I've never had the privilege of giving birth, so I don't know from first-hand experience the joy that being a mother can give. But I know the love I feel for the children and grandchildren that I gained when Edgar and I married. What a gift they are. I tell you, Fred, I don't know that I could manage it if my love for them were any stronger. If your grandmother's love for you was remotely like the love I feel, then I can promise you that even this number of years later, her love is strong enough to carry you through this project."

Fred bowed his head between his forearms and paused for several seconds. He looked at Edgar, then at Marcella. "What do you need me to do?"

Marcella sighed as privately as she could. "I wonder if you might have a stage play or maybe a musical that you've never produced publicly."

"Oh, there are dozens, most of them stored away in a dusty storage room."

"Are any of them fun little romantic plays?" Marcella asked.

Fred thought for a moment, shuffling his feet. "There is one that might not be too difficult to produce on short notice. How much time would we have?"

"Less than two months." Edgar said.

"Ouch." Fred said, squinting into the future. "Such time restraints would make almost any play impossible to properly produce."

"If the entire community pulls together and helps you,

would that one be simple enough to do within that time span?" Marcella asked.

"I believe so. It's a short play I wrote thirty or forty years ago titled *An Evening in April*. There are only three or four principal characters. If I had help with props and music and enough imaginative people who were fast learners to play the lead roles, I could probably make it work. I would need a young adult couple and one or two older citizens."

"That's wonderful," Marcella said, her eyes gleaming. "You write a list of the people and things you need—actors, carpenters, seamstresses, building supplies or whatever else, and we'll see that you have them."

"I think you might have forgotten about one thing," Fred said.

"What's that?" Edgar asked.

"A venue. Where could we possibly present such a performance in this community? We'll need a stage and dressing rooms and space for idle props."

"We'll find a venue," Marcella and Edgar said.

"I do so hope I don't let you down," Fred said. "I really hope I don't . . ." His voice trailed away.

———

MICHAEL WAITED FOR CECIL GREY TO PAY FOR HIS BOTTLE OF shampoo and two packs of gum, then took his place at the pharmacy checkout counter.

"Excuse me while I get this," Linda Cruz said as she grabbed the ringing telephone. She stood with her back to the counter for two or three minutes.

Michael picked up a Chapstick and read the label, then a copy of *Farmers Almanac*. Next to the register the back of a business card caught his attention. "Jason, air conditioning guy," it said in cursive hand-writing. "Call next time."

"Hey, Michael. What can I get for you?" Linda asked.

"Uh." He placed the Almanac back in the stack where he'd found it. "Sorry, Granny needs something for a sick headache. Whatever brand she bought last time, she said."

Linda retrieved a bottle from a shelf behind her and rang it up.

"Say, how about dinner this evening?" Michael said.

"I'm so sorry, but I've got to go into Huntsville as soon as I close. I hope that's okay."

"Yeah, it's no problem. I know it's short notice. Just thought I'd ask."

"I appreciate the offer just the same. Maybe we can try again another time," Linda said.

"Sure. Sure thing." Michael stuffed the pill bottle into his pants pocket and headed for the door. *Jason, the air conditioning guy. And what else?*

———

ON THE FRONT PORCH OF BROWN'S GENERAL STORE, OLLIE Smith, Grumpy, and Abe Jones tried to out-whittle Dave Crabtree. Dave was a champion whittler and had the trophies to prove it. Jesse and Edgar leaned against the porch rail, watching.

"Which of you are carpenters?" Edgar asked.

"Depends on what you call carpentering," Ollie said. "If you're talking about building houses and stuff like that, you'd be talking about Bull Brown. Don't know that you've ever met him, but he's Henry's second cousin. Lives down near Gurley. But now, if it's fences or hog pens—anything like that —well I'd probably be the one you'd need to see."

"What are you needing built?" Grumpy asked.

"We're going to need a white picket fence about twenty feet long and three scaled down houses, but just the fronts of them," Edgar said. "And if we can't find them already built, we'll need a picnic table and a porch swing."

"Why in the tarnation are you going to need the front of three houses?" Ollie asked.

"Actually it's not I who needs them. It's we who need them."

"Have you been talking to Marcella?" Grumpy asked.

"I'd say the odds are better than good, since he's married to her," Abe, the town gardener said.

"Okay, dumb question," Grumpy said. "But whatever this is that Edgar's talking about smells a lot like something Marcella would have her hand in."

"I confess. I have been talking to Marcella and the two of us have been talking to someone else who has agreed to help us with the entertainment for the fundraiser," Edgar said.

"That right there's great news," Ollie said. "I've been about worried sick thinking I'd got us all in over our heads here."

"It's going to take all of us pulling together to make this happen," Jesse said.

"You said us," Grumpy said. "Are you staying in town to help us?"

"I am," Jesse said.

"Well, what is this entertainment that's going to require so much work?" Henry asked.

Edgar looked at Jesse who returned the look. "Morgan Crossroads is going to put on its first ever professionally produced play," Edgar said.

The whittling stopped. Ollie dropped his knife on the floor. Grumpy and Dave Crabtree sat with their mouths open.

Neither Edgar nor Jesse said anything, but chose to let the idea simmer, or boil, whichever it turned out to be.

When the breathing resumed, Dave Crabtree said, "That sounds like one doozy of a job."

"Where in the world did you come up with that idea for entertainment?" Ollie asked.

"I don't mean any disrespect by this, Edgar, and I hope you know that, but this has got to be one of the most off the wall ideas I've ever heard, especially coming from somebody as smart as you," Grumpy said.

"There's nobody in this area that I know of with the experience to do anything like that," Abe Jones said.

"Well, we have a special guest who has agreed to stay around for a few weeks to help us with it," Edgar said.

"Who might that be?" Ollie asked.

"His name is Fred Starnes," Edgar said. "Frederick Starnes is his full name.

"He ain't that Starnes fellow you bought your house from, is he?" Ollie asked.

"The same," Edgar said. "I've checked into his background and his credentials."

"And he's very well qualified to produce the play," Jesse said.

"If I remember right, you're a literature professor, aren't you," Abe asked.

"Yes. And I promised Fred I would stay here until the performance is over."

"Okay," Henry Brown said, his forehead wadding into a near permanent crease. "What's the name of this play?"

"*An Evening in April,*" Edgar said.

"Never heard of that one," Grumpy said.

"Lord, I sure hope it's not one of those where every other word is thee or thou," Dave Crabtree said.

"Wherefore art thou, Romeo?" Henry waxed eloquent.

"No, men. There'll be none of that," Edgar said. "It's a modern play telling a modern story."

"So where does the carpenter work come in?" Grumpy asked.

"Sets and props," Jesse said.

"We promised Fred we would do our best to help him present a professional quality performance. That means we need the best, most realistic stage props we can build," Edgar said.

"I know this whole fundraising idea was one that us men drummed up, but it's starting to sound a little lop-sided," Ollie said.

"Oh, no," Edgar said. "The women are going to have to work just as hard as we are."

"Have you ever paid attention to the curtains and dresses and such as that in a play on television?" Jesse asked.

The men grunted. Some nodded.

"The women have to create from scratch, all the curtains, clothes, and decorations for the set. I promise they'll work as hard or harder than we will," Jesse said.

"*An Evening in April*," Henry said. "Sounds like one of those sappy love stories."

"You'll be proud of it," Edgar said. "We all will."

CHAPTER TWENTY-ONE

Dora Mae leaned as far over the pharmacy counter as her five-foot-tall body allowed, but not nearly as far as her nosiness prodded her to go.

"Did you lose something?" Linda Cruz asked from the aisle behind Dora Mae.

Dora Mae jerked and teetered backward, hanging her purse on the rotating rack of reading glasses and pill boxes. Before she could gather herself and steady the rack, two dozen pairs of glasses lay on the floor. Scattered around her feet was an assortment of breath mints, candy bars, and chewing gum that had flown off the shelf behind her when the eye glass rack fell into it.

Linda used one hand to steady Dora Mae and the other to upright the rack. "Are you okay?"

"Oh my," Dora Mae said with a slight crackle in her voice. "What have I done?"

"Did you find what you were looking for?" Linda asked.

"Probably not," another voice answered behind them. Eva Jo surveyed the wreckage, a fist propped on each hip. "But it looks like she went down trying."

Linda fought back a snicker.

Dora Mae straightened her skirt, retrieved her purse from the wayward rack, and said, "What is that supposed to mean, Eva Jo Clomper?"

Linda, having heard rumors that Eva Jo disliked anyone calling her by her full name, raised an eyebrow but said nothing.

"If you hadn't been halfway across the counter when Linda caught you, maybe you wouldn't have made such a mess."

"I was not. It was just a slight mis-step." Dora Mae squinted her eyes in Eva Jo's direction. "How would you know anything about what happened here?"

"Honey, I may be half as old as dirt, but I'm a long way from blind. I was standing out there on the sidewalk watching you through the window. And Honey, I'm telling you, it was like catching Henry Brown that time when he was eight or ten years old sneaking in Lida Joy Thrumpit's window, God rest her soul. All I could see was your rear-end and the soles of your shoes about to leave the floor. Plus, I bet Stella heard the racket all the way down at the cafe."

"Did you lose something behind the counter?" Linda asked.

"I was just...I thought I..." Dora Mae sighed. "No, I don't suppose I did."

"Why in the world were you taking yourself over Linda's counter?" Eva Jo asked. "You could've walked three steps standing straight up and been back there."

"What can I do for you?" Linda asked.

Eva Jo elbowed Linda and half whispered in her ear. "I bet you a dollar to a hole in a donut she was prying around to see what you and your love life have been up to."

"Dora Mae!" Linda said.

"I was doing no such thing," Dora Mae said.

"You know *The Whipper County Gazette* is due out tomorrow. She's probably scouting around for something juicy to write," Eva Jo said.

"Well, I have no idea why you'd come here looking for anything juicy to report. And especially about my love life."

"Okay, okay." Dora Mae lifted her hands in surrender. "I might have been looking for a certain piece of evidence to support a tip that someone gave me."

"What tip? What someone?" Eva Jo asked.

"Eva Jo, you know good and well that I never disclose my sources. I've worked very hard over the years to develop a group of people willing to help me put out the most pressing news stories in the Gazette."

"Yes, and most of those sources are in your head," Eva Jo said.

"Well, I assure you there is nothing newsworthy going on in this pharmacy," Linda said. "Whoever slipped you that tip was mistaken."

"Don't let it get under your skin, Honey," Eva Jo said. "Look on the bright side. You've been officially initiated into citizenship in Morgan Crossroads, Alabama. Folks tend to look on people as outsiders until they've made Dora Mae's list."

"Oh, Eva Jo. Would you kindly stop misleading Linda? Remember, she is an official member of the Rose Bud Circle," Dora Mae said.

Eva Jo gave Linda a slight side hug. "She's trying to get you married off."

"That's not true," Dora Mae said. "Not entirely. I'm simply trying to confirm that you have been invited to have the lead role in a play somewhere."

"A lead role? In a play? What play?" Linda asked.

"My source tells me you and some lucky man are to be the lead characters in a huge theatrical production."

"Where is this production, as you call it?" Eva Jo asked. "I might want to try out for it."

"I have it on good authority that it will be in Huntsville, possibly at one of those big churches," Dora Mae said.

"I can assure you that I'm not a lead actress in anybody's production. I haven't been in a play since I played Mother Goose in the third grade," Linda said.

"Dora Mae, you ought to be ashamed of yourself. You really should," Eva Jo said.

"If that's what you came to ask, what did you hope to find behind the counter?" Linda asked.

"Your copy of the script. I was sure you were spending every waking minute reading your lines. You know, memorizing them, like when Romeo memorized how to kiss Juliet."

Linda laughed. Eva Jo joined her.

Dora Mae gathered her well-worn dignity and, with her nose pointing somewhere on the ceiling, headed toward the door.

Polly parked Jewell Crabtree under the hairdryer and left her to read *People Magazine* for a while.

"So, who do you think Fred Starnes will pick to play the lead characters?" Gertrude Gleaves asked.

"What's the title of the play?" one of the Pearle twins asked.

"*An Evening in April*, according to Henry," Polly said.

"That sounds so romantic," the other Pearle twin said. "You don't suppose it takes place in Paris, do you?"

"I wouldn't think so," Gertrude said. "This is Morgan

Crossroads, Alabama, and except for Edgar and Marcella on their honeymoon, nobody around here has ever been to Paris."

"I went to Paris, Tennessee once when I was young," Polly said.

"Doesn't count," Gertrude said.

Polly, Gertrude, and the twins turned toward the door when it opened. Marcella walked in and sat in the only available chair. Before the door latched behind her, Eva Jo walked in and without closing the door, walked straight to the dryer and lifted it, still running, from Jewell's head.

"Looks like Eva Jo's on a mission," Gertrude said.

"You all listen up. I'm going to see what I can do to get Dora Mae Crawford committed," Eva Jo said.

"Committed?" Marcella asked. "What has she done to wind you up so?"

"The woman has lost her mind. Or, she's been watching too much television," Eva Jo said as she lowered Jewell's dryer.

"Pour yourself a cup of coffee," Polly said. "And let's hear it."

"There is no way on this earth that I could have made this up, so you all will know that what I'm telling you is the truth." Eva Jo hauled in a deep breath.

"Shoulders back," Marcella said, looking at Eva Jo.

Eva Jo did as Marcella suggested.

"Now, breathe slowly a couple times."

"I'm fine. I'm fine now," Eva Jo said.

"I don't believe I've ever seen Eva Jo in such a state," one of the Pearle twins said.

"It was bloomer city," Eva Jo said, throwing both hands in the air as if holding back applause. "I'm telling you, Dora Mae has completely outdone herself this time."

"Now, that's saying something, you know," Polly said.

"That's the truth if I ever heard it," Gertrude said. "She'd have to jump way off the deep end to beat some of the things I've known her to do."

"What has she done?" Marcella asked.

Eva Jo told of her walking on the sidewalk in front of Crossroads Pharmacy. "It was the funniest thing I've ever seen that woman do. All I could see was her old-lady drawers shining from the top of the counter and the bottoms of her shoes flailing around." Eva Jo held her hand to her chest as she shook in laughter. "Looked like the broad side of a goat hung up on a fence."

"Eva Jo!" Marcella slapped her hands across her chest.

"Well, it's true," Eva Jo said.

"Was she hurt?" Marcella asked.

"Only her pride and her reputation with Linda Cruz."

Polly turned off Jewell's dryer. "You're saying she was going over the counter? Why do you reckon she did that?"

"Let me guess. She was working on a story," Jewell said.

"That's what she claimed," Eva Jo said. "According to her, one of her unknown sources had informed her that Linda was going to play a lead role in some play in Huntsville. But I'll tell you what she was really doing."

"In Huntsville? Where did she get that idea?" Marcella asked.

"Maybe she went sleepwalking and woke up in Huntsville," Polly said.

"Who knows the truth?" Gertrude said. "But if I were a gambling person I'd bet she was spying on Linda."

One of the Pearle twins said, "That makes no sense. Linda is an absolute sweetheart."

"Why would she spy on her?" the other twin asked.

"She claimed she was looking for a copy of a script, but

here's what I think." Eva Jo said. "She's afraid she's going to lose out on finding Linda a husband. She thought she'd find some guy's phone number written somewhere behind that counter, then try to start something with it."

"Well, is Linda even going to be in the play?" Gertrude asked. "Not that it matters."

"And if she is, what would that have to do with finding her a husband?" Jewell asked.

"I think Linda would be perfect for the play, from what little I've heard," Marcella said. "But that decision will be up to Fred Starnes."

"Maybe somebody should call the sheriff and file charges on her," Eva Jo said.

"File what charges?" Marcella asked.

"Impersonating a reporter, that's what," Eva Jo said. "Or maybe impersonating a detective, like she thinks she's what's her name on *Murder She Wrote*."

CHAPTER TWENTY-TWO

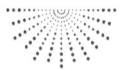

Stella refreshed Ollie's coffee and Henry's orange juice. "How about some more hash browns? Looks like you fellas are hungry."

"I'm fine," Henry said, holding his hand over his plate.

"I'll take some. Make 'em crispy around the edges," Ollie said.

Stella patted Henry on the shoulder. "I'll bring a little extra in case Henry changes his mind."

Ollie emptied two packs of sugar in his coffee and stirred it. "Did you ever feel like you'd bit off about two truck-loads more than you could chew?"

"You mean other than getting married?" Henry asked with a grin.

"Yep. Like this whole fund raising thing. What do either one of us know about putting on plays?

"Very little," Henry said. "Nothing, really."

"Same here. Last time I can remember us having a play around here, we had that Christmas one ten or fifteen years ago," Ollie said. "And it didn't go over too good. We wound up not having anybody in it but Mary and Joseph and Jesus."

TOM BUFORD

"I remember that," Henry said. "We started out with all the wise men and angels. But then we figured out there wouldn't be anybody left to watch it but the preacher, and he already kinda knew how the story went."

"Look, this whole thing started with me trying to outdo those women. You know, beat them at their own game." Ollie slurped his coffee. "But from what I'm feeling right about now, I'd say it might have backfired on us."

Henry pushed his plate aside to make way for the hash browns he hadn't asked for. "Oh, I don't know that I'd call it a backfire, but I admit it ain't going quite like I expected."

"We've got so much stuff collected for the yard sale that it's going to turn into a street sale. There's not a yard in Morgan Crossroads that could hold all that junk." Ollie started toward his mouth with an overloaded fork of hash browns, then stopped in mid-air, as if having second thoughts. He dunked them in ketchup and waved them around in a circle, pointing out the entire neighborhood. "And what about having enough people to do all that needs doing? We're going to have to borrow some guys from Porterville or Scottsboro or somewhere."

"Hadn't thought about it that way," Henry said. "From the way Edgar and Jesse are talking, there'll be a lot for us to do getting that play put on. I'm guessing Fred Starnes is going to have both of his hands full, so he wouldn't be available to collect money or park cars or serve cold drinks and cookies for the sale."

"The way I've got it figured, we'll have to get those ladies involved, too. I mean besides making curtains and stuff for the play," Ollie said.

"Don't quite seem right, does it?" Henry said. "Asking the women to help us beat them."

"Man, can you imagine all the jibber jabber that's going

on in that beauty shop? Between Dora Mae and Eva Jo and Polly, I don't see how we've got much of a chance of coming out of this in one piece," Ollie said.

———

FRED STARNES HAD AGREED TO PRODUCE THE PLAY IF A suitable venue was available and if he could have final say in anything that he thought might affect the performance. That included props, fabric, lighting, and other things. He borrowed Edgar's car and left early to scout for materials, props, and other necessities. Marcella had suggested he stop at Scottsboro's First Monday sale around the square and a few other places she knew of within a reasonable driving distance.

Jesse helped Edgar clean and straighten the garage and in the process gathered several items to add to the yard sale.

"You fellows did quite a job. Perhaps you could add the kitchen to your list," Marcella said.

"Maybe next week," Edgar said with a wink toward Jesse.

"I've had a grand idea," Marcella said. "I hope you didn't have plans of your own because I told Linda Cruz we'd meet her at Lucy's Cafe at noon for lunch. Is that alright with you two?"

Jesse looked at Edgar. Edgar shrugged and said, "Sure, why not?

"Great! Who's driving?"

"I am," Edgar and Jesse said.

CHAPTER TWENTY-THREE

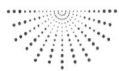

"I want it to be the same color as Lucille Ball's. Do you have that color?" Dora Mae asked.

"You're already a redhead," Polly said. "Why would you dye your hair just to be a little more red?"

"I'm planning an important meeting. I need it to be the same color and the same style as Lucy's."

"Why in the world would you change your hair color and go through all that just for a meeting?" Gertrude Gleaves asked. "Just iron your blouse real good and make sure you don't step in anything between your house and the meeting."

"Gertrude, I'm surprised at your attitude," Dora Mae said.

"Okay, Dora Mae. Where is this meeting going to be?" Polly asked.

"I'm not exactly sure yet."

"So you're still planning it," Gertrude said.

"Well, not exactly," Dora Mae said.

"Let me get this straight," Polly said. "You're dying your hair the color of Lucille Ball's."

"And she wants it styled like Lucy's." Gertrude said.

"Yes, that, too," Polly said. "You want your hair to look

like Lucy's so you can go to a meeting that you're not exactly planning and you don't exactly know where it's going to be. Have I got that right?"

"Yes, that's what I need from you."

"Dora Mae, have you looked in the mirror lately?" Gertrude asked.

"Of course I have. What kind of question is that?"

"It's the kind of question that comes before this one. Do you realize that you look about as much like Lucille Ball as Robert Redford looked like John Wayne?"

"What's that supposed to mean, that I'm not pretty?" Dora Mae asked.

Polly handed Dora Mae a box of tissues. "You might need these. It has nothing to do with you being pretty or not. But you can do your hair up anyway you want and nobody's going to mistake you for Lucy."

"Oh, I don't expect anyone to mistake me for Lucy. She's not alive anymore and I am," Dora Mae said.

"Let's back up to the beginning," Gertrude said. "Who are you planning to visit with when you have your important meeting?"

"I'm not at liberty to say. I haven't approached him about it yet."

"Ah-ha," Polly said. "You're trying to impress a man, and you think he likes Lucille Ball. Am I right?"

"It depends upon what you mean by trying to impress a man. If you think I have eyes for any man in this county, you'd be very wrong."

"What if he's not from Whipper County," Gertrude asked.

"You'd still be wrong. I might hope to inspire in this person the willingness to answer some confidential questions," Dora Mae said. "And that is the end of it. Now, can you make me look like Lucy or not?"

"HERE YOU ARE," STELLA SAID AS SHE SET THE CHEESEBURGER and onions rings in front of Jesse. "One cheeseburger, all the way. Best burger this side of the Mississippi."

Jesse stared at his plate, then at the roast beef dinners that Marcella and Edgar had ordered and the chef salad in front of Linda Cruz. "Wow, how many cows did it take to make this thing? I didn't remember these burgers being this big. I think you might have given some Texans a run for their money."

"My papa was from Texas. He did everything in a big way," Stella said. "Enjoy."

Just as Jesse bit off the first bite of burger, a hand patted him on the back. He tried to look up and greet the person, but couldn't without embarrassing himself.

"Quite a mouthful, isn't it," Eva Jo said. "Take it slow and easy. You'll eventually get it down."

Edgar greeted Eva Jo and Michael and looked around the table. "We could scoot over and make room for you if you'd like to join us." Then he felt something pointed bumping his shin, something that could only have been Marcella's shoe.

"That's okay," Michael said. "We'll sit over here." He and Eva Jo found a table in an opposite corner.

"On second thought, maybe this table is too small for six adults," Edgar said.

Marcella smiled.

Across the room, Eva Jo and Michael sat so that Michael's back was toward the other table and Eva Jo had an unobstructed view of it and its occupants.

"You knew they'd be here, didn't you?" Michael asked.

"No sir, I didn't," Eva Jo said.

"You had to know, Granny. You just can't make up timing like this."

"Well, I didn't know. What are you all stirred up about, anyway? I thought you'd dropped the idea of you and Linda Cruz getting anything going."

"I didn't say that," Michael said. He pointed a fork full of salad across the table toward Eva Jo. "You kept pushing me on about her and I quit talking about her. Besides that, I asked her out for dinner and she said she couldn't."

"Couldn't when? Right then or forever? Life's too short to drag things out when the competition's hot," Eva Jo said.

"What competition are you talking about? The guys trying to get something going with Linda, or the grannies in the Rosebud Circle conniving and trying to outsmart each other?"

"If you're interested in a life with Linda Cruz, you'd better step your game up a tad." Eva Jo leaned slightly to one side for a clearer line of view. "If the smile on Linda's face says anything, I'd say you better find something at that drug store that need's fixing."

DORA MAE PLACED HER BREAD AND EGGS ON THE CHECKOUT counter at Haley's Grocery. "What gift do you bring to a man who you want to interview for sensitive information?" she asked.

Lorraine Haley stood still, mesmerized by the hairdo in front of her.

"Honey, are you alright?" Dora Mae asked.

Lorraine blinked, as if snapped back into reality from a dream. "Yes, of course, I'm fine. I was just admiring your–"

"You can thank Polly for my new look. How do you like it?"

"It's, it's, well, it's just—"

"I told Polly that people would love it, and now I know I'm right."

"Did you ask me something, Dora Mae?" Lorraine asked.

"Yes, I did. What sort of gift do you bring to a man who you hope to have a dinner meeting with?"

"What kind of dinner meeting? A date?"

"No! Not a date. Just a dinner meeting. The sort of meeting you have when you're trying to gather sensitive information from a source," Dora Mae said.

A man behind her made a sound like a cross between a cough and a snort. Dora Mae turned to see Grumpy staring at her.

"Oh, it's you," Grumpy said.

"Of course it's me. Who did you think I was?"

"Don't know. I thought maybe we had a visitor in town. I don't think I've ever seen a head of hair like that, except maybe if my hero ever had a bad hair day. Except hers wasn't orange."

"And who's your hero? Wonder Woman?" Dora Mae asked.

"Phyllis Diller."

Dora Mae picked up the carton of eggs she'd laid on the checkout counter, hit Grumpy straight in the chest with it, then walked out with neither bread nor eggs.

LINDA CRUZ LEANED SLIGHTLY AND WAVED POLITELY AT someone across the room.

Marcella turned to see who was there. "Did a friend come in?"

"Not lately," Linda said. "I was just waving at Eva Jo. Several times I've noticed her looking this way. This time we made eye contact."

"She's just being Eva Jo," Edgar said.

"She seems to be very interested in what we're doing. Michael's been shaking his head a lot, and she's been leaning across the table talking to him."

"I'd just ignore her," Marcella said. "It's probably nothing more than her trying to figure out why Jesse ordered a burger instead of something else."

"She's really bothered about it, then," Linda said.

"We could all move to their table," Jesse said. "They're at the big table with several extra chairs."

"No, let's just finish our meals here," Marcella said. "Linda, did you grow up with the desire to be a pharmacist?"

Linda chuckled. "No, I had my heart set on becoming a history teacher until my senior year in high school."

"That's interesting," Jesse said. "What happened that caused you to change your focus to pharmacy?"

"I spent two weeks here in Morgan Crossroads with Uncle Robert during summer break before my senior year. We talked about careers and how the courses we took in school could impact our future. Biology had fascinated me during my junior year and after watching him work and hearing from him what he had to learn to become a pharmacist, I decided to study pharmacy instead of history. It didn't hurt that he promised to let me take over Crossroads Pharmacy when he retired if I would work hard and become a licensed pharmacist. And here I am," she said, spreading her arms as if presenting herself to the world.

"Well, you're doing a fine job, Linda," Marcella said.

"Isn't she, Edgar?"

Edgar agreed.

"Jesse's a professor of literature," Marcella said, gesturing toward him. "Why don't you move to Morgan Crossroads, Jesse? I understand there may be an opening at the new high school."

There was a moment of hesitance then Jesse said, "I thought about moving down here."

Marcella smiled and inched forward in her chair.

"But I decided to stay where I am for a while. Who knows what life will bring down the road?"

Marcella tried not to let her face reveal her disappointment.

CHAPTER TWENTY-FOUR

F RED S TARNES RETURNED FROM HIS PROP FINDING MISSION with the trunk and interior of Edgar's BMW packed with wall hangings, lamps, and material for curtains and costumes.

"Where shall I put these?" Fred asked. "A truck will be here tomorrow with more."

"Oh, my," Marcella said. *How did I forget to arrange the venue?* "Can you just leave them in the car for a few minutes? I need to make a phone call."

"Reverend Downs, we'd like to use the sanctuary and church hall for an event." She explained how the play would benefit the community and suggested that the ladies mission group might even make a few dollars by selling refreshments during intermission.

"I don't see a problem with it. There's nothing on the calendar for the next two months that can't be shifted around a bit," the pastor said.

Marcella sighed in relief. "Mr. Starnes, let's take what you've brought to the hall at Morgan Chapel. You might call and have tomorrow's delivery sent there, also."

"That's fine. Thank you," Fred said. "I'd like to meet with the contenders for the leading role within the next two or three days if possible. Do you have their names and phone numbers?"

Marcella froze for a moment. "Leading roles? We haven't discussed the particulars that you're looking for. I assume you'll need a male and a female. How old should they be?"

"That's my fault. I should have told you. We'll need a female and a male, both preferably in their late twenties or early thirties. Size isn't important, though some other factors might be."

"Well, there's Michael Clomper and let's see," Marcella said, staring out the kitchen window. "There's Jesse."

"Jesse said he'd rather help in the background than in an acting role," Edgar said. "How about Grumpy?"

"Oh, I don't know about him," Marcella said. "I've never thought of him as the theatrical type. He did play Scrooge in the sixth grade Christmas play one year, though."

"Who have you considered for the lead female role?" Fred asked.

"There's only one that I can think of at the moment who's in that age group. That's Linda Cruz," Marcella said. "Edgar, are you sure Jesse wouldn't be interested in auditioning?"

FRED STARNES AND MARCELLA STOPPED AND SPUN THEIR heads around to see whose car might be screeching to a halt in front of the church.

Fred looked at the little red car with an expression that might have said *where's the rest of it*? "Who is that?"

Marcella recognized the car but couldn't respond before

Dora Mae flung herself through the decorative iron gate and into the church courtyard.

"Dora Mae, is everything okay? Did your car break down?" Marcella asked.

Dora Mae glided right past Marcella and brought her size five shoes to a halt so that her forehead and blazing red Lucy hair were right below Fred Starnes's chin.

"Dora Mae, you might remember Mr. Starnes," Marcella said.

"Aren't you Fred Starnes?" Dora Mae asked. "I think we met briefly when you lived in Marcella's house."

"I'm sorry, ma'am," Fred said. "I never had guests when I lived here. You must be mistaken."

"Oh, we didn't meet in your home."

Marcella tugged at the back of Dora Mae's blouse, nudging her backward, out from under Fred's nose.

"Thank you," Fred said, glancing toward Marcella.

"We met at the Dairy Bar down Main, past Haley's Grocery," Dora Mae said. "I'm Dora Mae Crawford, editor of *The Whipper County Gazette*. I'd love to buy lunch and perhaps work in a short interview at the same time."

"Mr. Starnes is very busy," Marcella said.

"So am I," Dora Mae said. "That's why this evening at dinner is the only time I have available for the foreseeable future."

"I am quite busy, Ms . . . I'm sorry, what did you say your name is?" Fred asked.

"Dora Mae Crawford. You can call me Dora Mae. How about I pick you up at five o'clock? At Marcella's house. We'll go somewhere nice and quiet so we can make the best of your time."

Fred looked at Marcella.

Marcella shrugged.

"Okay, I have no idea why you'd wish to interview me, but I can give you exactly forty-five minutes, no more. I like punctuality, Ms. Crawford."

Fred made sure the church door was closed and escorted Marcella through the front gate to her car.

CHAPTER TWENTY-FIVE

MICHAEL CLOMPER PARKED IN FRONT OF CROSSROADS Pharmacy just in time to see Linda Cruz flip the sign to open. He patted his hip and shirt pocket for his wallet and cell phone, aimed his gaze at the door, and took in a deep breath. He let it ease out through puffed cheeks. Had she seen him? He thought if she had, she'd at least have waved or smiled.

"Here goes," he half-whispered.

The bell hanging behind the door sounded off with its usual clang bang clang rattle. Linda craned her neck around the sunglasses display and waved. "Michael! Is that your truck out there?"

"It is. It took a while, but it's finally back in good condition. And just in time. I've about had it driving granny's old rattle-trap."

"I'm sure you have. There's one thing about that truck of hers. It won't let her sneak up on anyone," Linda said, smiling.

"No, there's no danger in that ever happening. Between her truck and her voice, there's no hiding for her," Michael said.

"Where did that come from?" Michael said, pointing to a glass-doored cooler in the rear corner.

I bought it last week. A guy from Huntsville installed it yesterday. "Let's see if it's working." Linda stepped over to the cooler and took a Double Cola from it. "It's cold. Would you like one?"

Michael moved closer to see the variety. "I'd like a root beer, I think."

"There you go," Linda said, handing a brown bottle to Michael. "It's on the house."

He twisted the top off and took a good swallow. "Wow, that's cold. Just right."

"What brings you in this morning? Anything special you're looking for?"

"Shaving cream and a razor."

Before he got the words out, Linda was on her way to the aisle where he'd find shaving equipment. "Will any of these work? Any certain brand you like?"

Linda picked up a can of shave gel. "This is gel, but it comes in a variety of scents." She scratched the scratch and sniff spot and held it to her nose. "This one has a faint scent, but I like it. You might like a different one better."

He took the can from her and took in a big whiff, hoping to smell whatever she'd smelled. "This one is fine. What's it called?" He held the can at arm's length and read the label. "Spiced cedar." He scratched the label again and inhaled. "I've never heard of that one."

Linda said. "It's new. That just came in two or three days ago." She looked on a higher shelf. "I believe there was an after-shave that went with it."

When she found the after-shave, Michael took it from her and grabbed a pack of razors.

They walked to the checkout counter. She rang up his

order and took his money. "Here you go. Fifty-two cents is your change."

They said nothing for a second or two.

Linda broke the silence. "I suppose you've heard the chatter about the play and Fred Starnes."

"Yep, sure have."

"What do you think about that? It seems like an enormous project for a bunch of inexperienced people to take on," Linda said.

He laughed. "I agree with you. Or at least from the rumors I've heard about it. But that's normal for Morgan Crossroads. Most projects around here turn out to be more than any of us can handle on our own. Or sometimes even with a group of people working on it."

Linda nodded. "You know how little birdies talk, I'm sure."

"Sure do. You get used to it when Eva Jo Clomper's your granny."

"I've heard several rumors about me," Linda said.

"Like what?"

"Like, I'm going to play the lead female role in the play, even though I have no idea what it is or what it's about."

"Who told you that?"

"Dora Mae started it, coming in here trying to sneak information that wasn't here in the first place. Later I heard that through a different branch of the grapevine."

"Well, are you going to be in the play?"

"Michael! I have no plans to be in anyone's play, at least until someone with some authority in the matter speaks to me about it."

"Sorry," Michael said. "I heard you, so I don't know why I asked that question."

"It's okay. Between the budding actress rumors and the

soon to be a bride rumors, I can't keep my ears on straight or my mind either."

He shoved his hands in his pockets and looked at his feet. "What's this about a soon to be a bride rumor?"

"I think you can put that one together yourself. Every time I have something done around here, there seems to be a race between the older ladies around here to see if I need their favorite young man's help."

"Well, do you? I mean, do you need their help? And please don't take that question wrong," he said when he saw Linda plant both fists on her hips. "I'm asking because Granny is about to drive me nuts with that same thing. I don't think she'd want me to say this, and she's denied it from the beginning, but I think she and Marcella and Dora Mae, and . . ."

He pointed through the wall toward Main Street, raising his voice as he shook his finger. "And all those ladies that keep those chairs full at Polly's House of Beauty have a contest going."

"A contest?" Linda half-shrieked.

"Yes, a contest. Don't ask me what the prize is supposed to be, other than maybe one of them just out-doing the others and whatever satisfaction they get from that."

"Is that why you came over to help me with the awning?" Linda asked.

"No, not for my part, it wasn't. I'm embarrassed to say this, but I needed to earn a little money, and that was something I could do. But then–"

"Then your grandmother got involved," Linda said.

"That's putting it lightly," Michael said. "She's about driven me nuts trying to push me into seeing you."

"Does that mean asking me out for dinner was Eva Jo's invitation and not yours?" Linda asked.

"No! No, it wasn't. I asked you out because I wanted to

ask you out. I wanted to get to know you better. But she started trying to pressure me into getting over here with first one excuse, then another."

"I see," Linda said, deep in thought. "Ask me out to dinner tonight. Go on, ask me."

Michael stammered and struggled to get a deep breath. "Ask you out? For tonight?"

"Yes. Go ahead. Ask me."

"Okay, would you have dinner with me this evening?"

"I'd be happy to, with one condition."

"What condition," Michael asked.

"That we dress up and we go to Lucy's Cafe. Six o'clock. Center table. I'll be dressing up. Maybe you can, too."

The bell over the door went through its clanging serenade again as Michael left and Dora Mae entered.

"What was he smiling about?" Dora Mae asked.

"Who? I didn't notice anyone smiling," Linda said. "It's a pretty day out today. Maybe that's why."

CHAPTER TWENTY-SIX

At 4:59 sharp, Dora Mae rang the bell at Marcella's front door.

Marcella peeked through the sidelight and opened the door. "Come in," she said, holding her open hand out toward the entry hall.

"Thank you," Dora Mae said. "Is Mr. Starnes ready? I do like punctuality, you know."

"He's in the family room, waiting for you. Let's see if he's ready to leave." The ladies walked down the hall with Dora Mae right on Marcella's heels.

"Mr. Starnes, your five o'clock appointment is here," Marcella said.

It was hard to decide which was more over-dressed for the occasion. Fred Starnes wore a tailored Italian suit and shoes, whose brand names only he could have pronounced. Then, there was Dora Mae with her Lucy hair riding high above a blinding red, yellow, and blue floral dress which hovered over white patent leather pumps.

Edgar fought the idea that he should stay silent, but lost. "Well, you two will certainly light up Main Street."

Marcella elbowed Edgar as inconspicuously as she could. "Dora Mae, where are you taking Mr. Starnes for dinner?"

"I thought we'd try the Dairy Bar," Dora Mae said.

Fred twitched, or at least Marcella thought he had.

"Won't it be a bit loud there for an interview?" Marcella asked. "There's no inside seating and the young people like to hang out there."

"Oh, I guess I didn't think that one through as thoroughly as I should have," Dora Mae said.

"How about Lucy's?" Edgar asked.

"Too many inquisitive ears there," Dora Mae said. "If we eat there, the story will be old news before I have time to print it."

Fred Starnes followed the conversation from one person to another and back, looking as if he'd prefer walking barefoot across a ten-lane freeway in Los Angeles. At rush hour.

Edgar said, "Dora Mae, you might drive over to Porterville, but by the time you get there, both restaurants will be full. Why don't you just take a chance on Lucy's Cafe?"

"That's a great idea," Marcella said. "Lucy's shouldn't be too busy this time of the week. It would be your quietest option and, if you go on right away, you'll still be able to get a quiet corner table."

"What do you think, Mr. Starnes?" Dora Mae asked. "I don't want you to be inundated with autograph seekers and all. You know, we don't get celebrities through here too often."

Fred straightened his lapels and clasped his hands. "I'm certainly no celebrity and I've never had anyone anywhere ask for my autograph. I'm sure that won't change just because I'm spending a few weeks in Morgan Crossroads, Alabama." He made sure he'd properly tucked his tie inside his buttoned suit coat. "I rather expected we'd have dinner at a restaurant with indoor dining."

"You two'd better get going," Marcella said. "It'll be 5:30 by the time you get to a table anywhere."

"Okay, Mr. Starnes, it appears there might have been just a slight oversight in my plans. We'll have dinner at Lucy's Cafe. I don't anticipate there'll be anyone there to interrupt our interview."

Fred Starnes excused himself and left the room for a minute.

Marcella drew up next to Dora Mae. "It's none of my business, Dora Mae, but why in the world did you intend to take someone like Mr. Starnes to the Dairy Bar, of all places?"

Dora Mae hesitated, then said, "If you must know, I had hoped to help him feel welcome in this little town by taking him somewhere he could have some home cooking."

"Home cooking?" Marcella asked in a muffled shriek that jerked her eyebrows into an arch. "At the Dairy Bar?"

"Well, yes. Their burgers taste almost just like the ones I try to make."

As if on cue, Fred Starnes returned, ready to go.

"Edgar, do you think we should have dinner at Lucy's, too?" Marcella asked.

"That's a different question than would I like to have dinner at Lucy's," Edgar said. "I can see all those tiny little wheels turning in your mind. What's going on?"

"I'm just thinking about poor Fred. What if Dora Mae is more than he can handle?"

"Don't you think Fred Starnes has been interviewed before? I'm sure he has for some of his productions."

"Yes, I'm sure he has. But I'm certain he's never been interviewed by the likes of Dora Mae Crawford."

"Point taken," Edgar said. "What is her goal in this interview? Do you have any idea?"

"I can only guess. She wants me to think she's just interviewing him about the production, but . . ."

"But what?"

"But I think it has very little to do with the production. I'd be very surprised if she's conversant enough in theatrical matters to ask intelligent questions on the subject," Marcella said.

"So, are we left to assume that she has her Sherlock hat on somewhere under that hair? Where did she get the idea for that hairdo, anyway?"

"Who knows? I heard she wanted to look like Lucille Ball for this interview. Heaven only knows why, though."

"I suppose we could drop in and have dinner. How would we know if he needed our rescue services? I expect Dora Mae will be speaking in her slightly above a whisper voice to protect her story from prying ears."

"I thought about that, too. Perhaps you could fall back on some of your attorney skills to see what was going on, just to be sure he wasn't in distress of any kind," Marcella said. "You know, read his lips or something."

"Marcella, dear, I'm not Perry Mason and I'm not a lip reader. You're more sensitive to people's emotions than I, so perhaps we should go by your judgement."

"Well, let me grab my purse. Maybe he'll feel better just knowing he has another way to leave if he should need it."

CHAPTER TWENTY-SEVEN

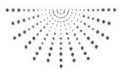

THERE WERE MORE CARS THAN USUAL SURROUNDING LUCY'S Cafe when Marcella and Edgar arrived. Inside, they found Fred Starnes staring across the table at the back of Dora Mae's Lucy hair.

Edgar placed his hand on Fred's shoulder and asked, "What is Dora Mae looking at?"

Fred shrugged. "I'm not certain, but she seems particularly upset that we were asked to move from the corner table to this one."

"Dora Mae, Honey, what's the matter?" Marcella asked.

No response.

Marcella stepped in front of Dora Mae, blocking her view of whatever she'd been obsessed with. "Dora Mae, what's the problem?"

"I'll tell you what the problem is. Stella had the audacity to tell us we couldn't have the corner table and moved us right here, dead in the center of the restaurant."

"Why couldn't you sit in the corner?"

"Well, look for yourself. Polly and Henry and whoever those other people are came in right after us. Stella took them right to our table and said Polly had reserved the table. Since when does Stella take reservations for tables? When?"

"Those are some of Polly's cousins. She'd been looking forward to their arrival for weeks," Marcella said.

Dora Mae pulled Marcella closer and in a half-whisper said, "How can I discretely interview Mr. Starnes with all this noise going on? I'll have to yell my questions at him and hope he hears them. Then—" She pointed toward the corner table. "Polly'll hear it and have it all told as soon as she gets back to the salon."

"They'll get it sorted out," Edgar said.

"I certainly hope so," Fred Starnes said. "I don't understand what she's so upset about. People request reservations for a reason. It's quite normal, actually."

"Well, not in Morgan Crossroads. At least, not yet."

Fred Starnes motioned Edgar to lean closer. "If I can be so rude, what is it about Ms. Crawford's hair? She's dyed it such a painfully bright color that I can hardly stay focused in a conversation with her."

"You'd have to ask her about that. Just go with it, if you can. My guess is that she'll change it back to her normal red hair before long."

Dora Mae turned around once she'd allowed the frustration to drain from her face. "Would you like some water, or perhaps some iced tea, Mr. Starnes?"

Fred motioned toward the table. "The waitress brought glasses of both while you were talking to Marcella."

Dora Mae looked around the table. "So, she did, and rolls, too." She patted her cheek, hoping the blush she felt rising wasn't visible.

"Edgar, let's sit over here," Marcella said, motioning toward the table by the front window.

LINDA CRUZ AND MICHAEL CLOMPER MET ON THE FRONT porch at Lucy's Cafe just before six o'clock.

"What's going on in there?" Michael asked. "Looks like half the county's here."

"I haven't heard of any parties," Linda said, looking inside to scan the crowd. "It looks like we're a little too late to grab the center table."

Michael joined Linda for a look through the front door. Stella, on her way somewhere with a tray of tea glasses, saw them and motioned them in.

He nodded toward the center table. "Is that who I think it is?" Michael asked, trying to overlook the wad of flaming red atop her head. "It is! Dora Mae has roped that Starnes fellow into having dinner with her. How'd she do that?"

"I don't know. I'll try to reserve judgment on that one," Linda said.

Inside, they took the only available table, one along the wall next to Marcella and Edgar. Stella stopped by with a water pitcher and two menus. "Here you go. Menus and water for two of Morgan Crossroads' finest looking young people."

"Thanks," Michael said.

"Thanks for the compliment," Linda said.

"No need to thank me. Just telling the truth," Stella said as she started away from the table. She hesitated and turned half way around. "No chicken fried steak this evening. Polly and her bunch wiped me out."

DORA MAE SPREAD A HEAVY LAYER OF MUSTARD AND KETCHUP on the bottom half of her buttered and grilled burger bun, then laid a thick slice of red onion to rest there, fingering it until it was perfectly centered. Two long slices of dill pickle, a well done handmade meat patty, and a hand-cut slice of cheddar cheese formed a perfect pedestal upon which to plant the seeded bun top. She leaned back to get a full side view of her creation, then felt her face fall. How was she going to shove a four inch thick burger into her petite mouth in any way that was socially acceptable?

Fred Starnes sprinkled vinegar and oil on his salad and requested a pepper mill. There being none available, he settled for a black plastic pepper shaker. He requested clarified butter for his Italian bread, but settled for the four pre-sliced margarine pats that Stella heated in a small dish on the grill. He'd hoped for veal parmigiana with grilled asparagus, but was happy to get lasagna and steamed broccoli.

Across the table, Dora Mae sat stupefied by the burger she'd built.

Fred straightened himself and his lapels. "Perhaps you could ask Lucille Ball how she would eat it."

Her cheeks warmed. "I don't think Lucy ever ate here. You do know that Stella advertises the best burger this side of the Mississippi, though."

"I read that on the sign. How would one know whether it was or wasn't if she couldn't bring herself to bite into it?" Fred said.

Dora Mae ventured a look toward Marcella's table just in time to see Marcella cut her eyes back toward her own plate. Edgar waved.

The noise at the corner table had quietened without Dora Mae noticing. When she glanced that direction, every person but one was staring at Dora Mae's burger. In an effort to regain control of the situation, she turned back toward Fred Starnes and saw Michael Clomper and Linda Cruz enjoying their roast beef and potatoes. They smiled and kept chewing.

Fred took a fork-full of salad and while it was on its way, he said, "Your burger's going to be cold soon."

"I'm sorry. I'm so embarrassed," Dora Mae said.

"Don't be," Fred Starnes said. "If I may offer a suggestion, perhaps you could take the meat out and eat it separately. Call it a ground beef steak, served with an onion, pickle, and cheddar sandwich."

"That sounds awful."

"Perhaps. But that is exactly what you have there. Just rearrange the parts and pay no attention to what anyone else thinks about it."

Dora Mae made the visual rounds again, trying to be inconspicuous. She smiled when Linda Cruz smiled and waved, and again when Edgar raised his fork to her. The sound coming from the corner table had raised to its former volume. She cut off a small portion of meat and followed it with a bite of her personally created onion, pickle, and cheddar sandwich.

CHAPTER TWENTY-EIGHT

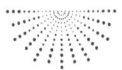

IT WAS CRUNCH TIME AT BROWN'S GENERAL STORE. ON AN average day, three rockers were enough to seat the men holding court there. But not for today's events. Henry and Ollie carried the old church pew from inside the store behind the wood stove out to the front porch. They, plus Grumpy, Edgar, Jesse, Cecil Grey, Abe the gardener, Michael Clomper, and Dave Crabtree wedged themselves in wherever they fit.

After a pause to allow a particularly loud log truck to pass under the traffic light, Fred Starnes relaxed as much as he could and spoke. "Gentlemen, thank you for meeting with me this morn—"

"Ain't no problem," Grumpy said, waving an open hand toward Fred.

"That's right," Ollie said before Grumpy had finished.

Edgar said, "We're just glad you've agreed to help us with our fundraiser."

Fred cleared his throat and loosened his tie.

"It's okay if you don't wear a tie around here," Abe, the

gardener said. "Nobody else wears one. Some of us have never owned one."

"Except Edgar," Henry said, pointing toward the farthest rocking chair. "I expect he's got a closet just for ties."

The porch filled with laughter and chatter, then quietened.

Fred passed a stack of papers to Grumpy and asked him to take one and pass them to the next person.

After each man received a copy Fred asked them to look at page two.

"Please overlook my poor drawing skills. I think you can still get an idea of the set props we'll need for the play we're producing. You'll see there are twelve pieces in total."

He explained how drawing number one showed the reverse side of the section in drawing number two. Number two was the inside corner wall section. Number one was the same piece, but finished on the opposite side as an exterior wall corner.

"Does anyone have a question?" Fred Starnes asked.

"According to the measurements on these drawings, these suckers are gonna be big," Ollie said.

"And heavy," Henry said.

"I don't have a clue how any of these are gonna help you put on a play," Grumpy said. "They just look like a bunch of pieces to me. Ain't a whole room among them, even if you stuck 'em all together."

Fred searched for a non-theatrical explanation.

"We won't need complete rooms," Jesse said, propping his elbows on his knees for a better look across the group. "Some scenes will just use one or maybe two pieces."

"I don't get it," Abe the gardener said.

"Have any of you ever seen a professionally produced play?" Fred asked.

Just two hands went up, Jesse's and Edgar's.

"The idea is not to present an entire room the way it appears on television," Fred said. "Theatrical performances are an art form that allows viewers to use their imaginations to fill in certain blanks. For example, you see in drawing number two a corner section of a living room, or parlor. There's a window on one short wall, a corner, then another short blank wall where there'll be hanging a painting or something of that sort."

"These will look different on stage with proper lighting," Jesse said. "That corner section may sit in the center of the stage. But because of black background curtains and the use of equipment that allows us to have just a light or two shining on that area, the viewer is better able to imagine the entire room."

"I think Mr. Starnes had some furniture pieces on his list of props." Edgar said. "I imagine there'll be a chair or a table with chairs in front of that corner wall where characters will act out their parts."

"Okay, I can picture that," Henry Brown said. "What I don't get is where we're gonna keep all the stuff that's not being used. You sure can't have all of this on that little stage at one time. There's barely room for a podium and that half a choir that stands up there every Sunday."

"Yeah. If we have these sections of rooms and other stuff hiding out off the stage waiting to be used in another scene, where's the audience going to sit?" Michael Clomper said.

Fred raised his hand with a rare smile across his face. "I can't tell you exactly how to do it because I'm not mechanically inclined. I couldn't tell you a thing about how to use power tools, so I'm depending on your skills to guide you in building what we need. For example, the drawing of that corner wall just represents an idea of what we need to see on stage. The part that isn't obvious in the drawings is that the large pieces will be built in small sections so we can bring in them through the side door at the front of the sanctuary and quickly assemble them on stage. Your ingenuity will make that happen."

"Are you talking about that dinky little side door up there by the organ?" Ollie asked.

"I don't know if it's ingenuity or not, but we're gonna have to come up with some real ideas to pull that off," Grumpy said.

The laughter started with Henry Brown and made its rounds all the way to Fred.

Michael Clomper turned to Edgar. "Do you have any idea how we're going to do that? I mean, what if it rains that day? How's this stuff going to stay dry while it's not needed?"

"Fred, tell me if I've got this right." Edgar scooted forward. "We'll divide the stage into two small areas, so we'll use both doors. The one on the left near the organ and the one on the right near the piano."

"That's right," Fred said.

Edgar continued. "While a scene's playing on the left side, a curtain will be drawn across the right side. While the curtain's closed, we'll carry in the pieces for the next scene and assemble them as quietly and quickly as we can."

"Then," Jesse said, "when the performance on the left side is finished, the curtain will close. The right side will open and the play will continue while we set up the left side for its next scene."

"What if it rains?" Michael asked.

"What about some large enclosed party tents?" Fred asked. "Does anyone in Morgan Crossroads have one?"

"The last party we had around here was when Marcella and Edgar got married. We didn't have a tent for that and it was just out in the parking lot over yonder at Lucy's Cafe," Ollie said.

"We'll rent one," Edgar said, scribbling a note. "No, two. We'll need one for each side."

"Let's eat," Grumpy said. "Who brought the sandwiches?"

"I did," Michael said. "Granny packed enough for us to all eat lunch two or three times. That is, except for something to drink. She said we'd have to worry about that on our own."

"That sounds like Eva Jo Clomper," Ollie said.

"Go in there and help yourselves to drinks," Henry said. "I just put some Double Colas and root beer in the cooler this morning. The coffee might be a little stout. It's left over from sausage biscuit time this morning."

"Whoa," Jesse said with eyes that shoved his eyebrows northward. "Look at this ham sandwich."

"How're you going to shovel that into your mouth?" Abe the gardener said.

"That looks like a New York deli sandwich," Fred Starnes said as he peered at the thin-sliced roast beef on his. "I'll show you."

CHAPTER TWENTY-NINE

"ARE YOU AND LINDA CRUZ GONNA GET SOMETHING GOING?" Eva Jo asked.

Michael looked up from the drawings in front of him. "I'd like to. What's the gossip line saying now?"

"What kind of question is that? Do you think I get all my questions from old ladies yakking out the top of their heads?"

"You don't really want me to answer that one, do you?"

"Doesn't matter if you do or don't. I heard you two were looking like a couple at Lucy's Cafe the other evening."

"And that's not gossip?" Michael asked.

"Not if it comes from somebody you can trust. If you hear it from Dora Mae, that would be gossip in its finest form. But I didn't hear it from her."

"Let me guess. Polly and Marcella." With his face toward Fred Starnes's set drawings, he peered out the top of his eyes.

"Nope. Try again," Eva Jo said with a proud smile.

"Okay. Last try. It had to be Stella or Edgar, and Edgar's not into gossiping."

"It was me," Eva Jo said, cackling. "I decided to let Stella and her bunch do the cooking because I was worn out from working on that fence all day. But there wasn't an empty table in the place. I didn't want to barge in on you and Linda, so I took myself down to the Dairy Bar and choked down a greasy chili dog and some greasier fries."

Michael dropped his pencil. "I'm not so sure you should've put yourself through that kind of torture just to cure a hunger pain, but I appreciate you not breaking in on our date."

"So it was a for real date," Eva Jo said, glowing and straightening herself.

"I guess you could call it that. Things didn't turn out like we planned, but we had a good time and good food, and the entertainment at the center table was worth the price of admission," Michael said.

"I saw Fred Starnes enduring Dora Mae's Lucy look. By the way, what kind of sandwich was she eating? Looked like a hamburger bun mashed around a slab of onion."

FRED STARNES SAT STRAIGHT ON A LADDER BACK WOODEN chair at a small table in Morgan Chapel with nothing more in front of him than a few copies of the play script, a notepad, and a pen.

Marcella and Jesse sat in seats behind him.

Two rows of eight folding chairs faced Fred. All were filled with people from Morgan Crossroads, Porterville, and other communities who were there to audition.

"Thank you for taking time out of your day to audition for roles in our upcoming play titled *An Evening In April*," Fred said. "The play is a short and simple three act production with just three main characters—a young lady, a young man, and an older uncle. There are two minor parts. In each chair, there is a white envelope containing a three page print out from the second act. I'll ask you now to remove the pages from the envelope and read your lines silently. Please take the next five minutes to read."

Marcella and Jesse, who had read the entire script, quietly read their copies of the audition section. Fred scribbled on his notepad, glancing over the group as he wrote.

"Okay, we'll start the auditions now, beginning with the front row. As you complete your audition, you may be excused. We'll be in touch with you within twenty-four hours if we choose you for parts in our production. For those who are chosen, rehearsals will begin Tuesday evening in this room."

Less than two hours later, the casting call was over. Like Fred, Marcella and Jesse had kept notes as people read their lines. Linda Cruz, Mary Beth from the flower shop, and one of the twins were among the female contenders. For the male lead role, Michael Clomper auditioned, as did a recently graduated high school football star from Porterville, Pastor Jeremiah Downs, and Grumpy. Several others read for the male parts, including an octogenarian exotic rose hobbyist from Scottsboro.

"Are you free this evening?" Fred asked Jesse and Marcella.

"Sure," Jesse said.

"Of course. What time?" Marcella said.

"Let's get together at seven o'clock," Fred said. "We need to select the cast as soon as possible."

POLLY'S HOUSE OF BEAUTY HAD TURNED INTO THE WAR ROOM for the sewing machine brigade.

"Did anyone see that stack of drawings that Fred Starnes handed out to the men?" Polly asked.

"I did," Marcella said. "They'll get it done, though."

"They'd better," Jewell said, "since they're the ones that started all this in the first place."

"How in the name of heaven are we supposed to get everything on this list sewn," one of the twins asked, raising her stapled group of drawings for show.

"One piece at a time," the other twin said.

"Not very original," Dora Mae said, "but true."

"How many sewing machines can we count on?" Polly asked.

"I have two," Marcella said.

"I've got one and Eva Jo said she has two," Polly said.

"One," both twins said.

Other hands went up.

"So that's nine machines," Lorraine Puckett said. "Where are we going to set them up?"

"Well, we could each take an assignment or two and sew them at home," Marcella said.

"It's a bit of a mess at the moment, what with all the news that's been happening lately," Dora Mae said. "But I could move my newspaper business into the bedroom for a few days and we could set up in my dining room."

"Now, that's a first," Polly said. "When has Dora Mae Crawford ever volunteered her home for anything?"

"Thank you, Dora Mae. That would be nice," Marcella said. "When shall we start?"

They hemmed and hawed until nine o'clock tomorrow won out.

"Don't forget to stop by the church hall and pick up the fabric for the pieces you're sewing," Marcella said.

"And pack a lunch," Jewell yelled over her shoulder on her way out.

"You won't need to pack a lunch," Polly said toward Jewell's back. "Eva Jo's keeping us and the men in food and refreshments for the day."

CHAPTER THIRTY

Ollie's barn, normally a large metal building full of tractors, was now a wood-working shop. The privilege had been granted because it was the only place in Morgan Crossroads that had the needed space and a concrete floor. There was Grumpy's welding shop and garage, but the floor had more grease on it than the walls had paint. No one thought that would work out too well.

The lumber yard in Porterville delivered lumber, drywall, paint, and other items. The men collected every sawhorse, table saw, and hammer they owned or could borrow and set them up in a semi-assembly line fashion.

On a long table borrowed from the church, Eva Jo had arranged an assortment of overloaded meat biscuits, fruit, sliced bread beside a toaster, and a platter of homemade sticky cinnamon rolls. On the floor was a large ice chest she'd filled with a variety of drinks to wash down the food.

They had elected Edgar to the role of supervisor because his talents lay more in reading and understanding detailed drawings and plans than in executing them with power tools he'd never operated. It helped that several of his conversations with Fred Starnes had been about the detailed needs each individual piece would fulfill.

"Somebody answer a question for me," Grumpy said. "Let's say we get all these parts of imaginary rooms built, who's gonna do the painting and wallpapering?"

"What wallpapering?" Ollie said.

Henry stopped his saw half-way through the cut. "Nobody said anything about wallpapering."

"I don't believe there's any wallpapering to be done," Edgar said, scanning the papers he held. "It wasn't on the supply list or the list of skills we'd need to have."

"Well, ain't some of these walls supposed to be kinda frilly?" Grumpy asked. "You gotta have wallpaper to make up frilly."

"They sure don't need to ask me for any wallpapering help," Michael Clomper said. "I can barely make a straight line with masking tape."

Jesse chuckled and said, "Maybe the women have that on their list. They might approach it differently, maybe with something like lace curtains."

"I can live with that," Ollie said. "Bring on the lace."

Henry and the other men went back to sawing and nailing and painting. By mid-afternoon they'd built all the wall sections, including one with a tiny front porch complete with rails. There was even a battery powered porch light by the front door. Two wooden rocking chairs that Eva Jo had agreed to repaint and loan would fit perfectly on each side of the door.

"Michael, I thought for sure you'd wind up with the lead part in the play," Henry said. "At least that's what Polly thought, and I agreed with her."

"No, I didn't make it, but that's alright. I don't know who got the lady's part. But if anybody other than Linda Cruz got it, I'm not sure how I would have done, trying to talk all sweet to Mary Beth and stuff like that," Michael said. "Not that there's anything at all wrong with Mary Beth. She's nice and all that. I just don't know her as well as, you know, as well as–"

"As well as you know Linda Cruz," Jesse said.

"Yeah, that's it. I don't know her like I know Linda, and that might have turned awkward." Michael pointed at Grumpy. "But ole Grumpy, there, he made it. He gets to be the uncle in the play."

"Well, I'll be hornswoggled," Ollie said. "Who woulda ever thought we'd have a future celebrity out here in this barn sawing and nailing two by fours with us?"

Grumpy waved away the comments. "I'll never be any kind of celebrity. Come to think about it, I'm not too sure I even know how to spell it." He laughed.

"How'd you get the part in the play?" Ollie asked as he checked the smoothness of the cut he'd just made.

"I don't have a clue. I haven't done any acting except maybe in the church Christmas play when I was a kid or maybe in grade school. I don't know how to act. I just read those papers that Fred Starnes gave me and I reckon him and Marcella and Jesse liked the way I read."

"You did fine," Jesse said. "You're going to do an outstanding job being an uncle."

"THIS REMINDS ME OF MY OLD DAYS IN THE HOSIERY MILL. We'd sit there all day, surrounded by rows of sewing machines, sewing the legs on those pantyhose together," Jewell Crabtree said.

"Boy, do I remember those days," Polly said.

"I don't remember you ever working in the mills," Dora Mae said. "When did you ever work in a mill?"

"I didn't, but Momma did. She had to quit because of the way her hands hurt so bad."

Grumpy and Henry had come by that morning and cleared everything from Dora Mae's dining room except the dining table and china cabinet. Now, the room looked more like a commercial sewing shop than a place to have dinner.

The women had donated nine sewing machines for the day, some portables which sat on the dining table and some that were built into sewing cabinets. Those in cabinets sat along the walls wherever there was an electrical outlet. One sat unused. The twins sewed on two of them while other women sewed around the table. The machines rattled and clicked and hummed as rolls of fabric became curtains and dresses and skirts.

"Who took the measurements for these dresses?" Polly asked.

"I think it was Eva Jo, wasn't it?" Lorraine Puckett said.

"I did," Marcella said. "Why do you ask? Did I miss something?"

"It's just that these look pretty small to me. This one is supposed to be for the lead role."

"It is. That's the dress for the opening scene."

"Well, are you sure Mary Beth isn't a tad larger than this," Lorraine said.

"Oh, she isn't in the lead role," Marcella said.

"How did that happen?" Dora Mae asked.

"Someone else had a better audition," Marcella said.

"Does Fred Starnes know about this?" Dora Mae asked.

Every sewing machine in the room screeched to a halt. Every head turned in Dora Mae's direction as if on cue.

She shrugged and covered her mouth with the fingers of

both hands. "Of course, he would know. For a moment I forgot that he was at the auditions." She motioned around the room. "You can get back to sewing."

"Now, look what you did," Gertrude Gleaves said. "My bobbin thread broke."

"So, who got the lead role?" a twin asked.

"Linda Cruz will be playing the lead," Marcella said.

"Let's hurry and get done," Dora Mae said. "That's the biggest news to hit Morgan Crossroads, Alabama since Marcella got married. This news deserves a special edition of the *Gazette*."

"Not so fast," Eva Jo yelled from the kitchen. "I finally got those men fed. You all aren't leaving here until you eat this table full of salad and fancy sandwiches."

"This news about Mary Beth not being in the play has got me curious," Lorraine said.

"What's that," Polly said.

"How's that going to work out? You know, Linda Cruz playing Michael's love interest."

The second twin said, "Unless I'm missing something here, it's not Linda Cruz playing Michael's love interest or the other way around. It would be whichever character Linda is playing. And it wouldn't be Michael who is the love interest. That would be whatever his character's name is."

"Well, of course," Lorraine said. "But even so, it would have to be awkward for Michael to be flirting with Linda."

Eva Jo made her appearance, wiping her hands on her apron. "You're all worrying over spilled milk, anyway. Michael won't be flirting with Linda. Preacher Downs is."

Dora Mae tripped over her own feet trying to stand up from her sewing machine. Polly pricked her finger and drew blood when she lost control of a straight pin. Jewell went pale as though she'd just seen death walk through the door.

"What?" Eva Jo said. "You never heard of a preacher in a play?"

"But—but he's a minister," Polly said. "A reverend."

"He's a single reverend with great acting skills," Marcella said. "He'll be outstanding in that role. Did any of you know that he had studied to become an actor before he went to divinity school?"

"Well, no," Jewell said.

"Neither did I until after the auditions," Marcella said.

"I don't think anyone did," a twin said. "Someone would have talked about it by now if they'd known."

"But how is that going to look to all the strangers in the audience?" Dora Mae said. "I need to speak with Mr. Starnes about this. We just can't have a pretty young lady like Linda Cruz smooching on the preacher right up in front of everybody."

Polly said, "You might be carrying it a bit too far, Dora Mae. Unless he's introduced as the pastor, who's going to know? And what does a single man have to be embarrassed about anyway, sitting in a chair talking about the weather or whatever they're going to be talking about up there?"

"Listen to yourself, Polly," Dora Mae cupped her hands behind her ears. "Open your eyes. He doesn't have to introduce himself as the pastor. He wears a collar that tells the whole wide world who he is."

Eva Jo stepped next to Dora Mae and placed her arm around Dora Mae's waist. "Let me try to help you with this before somebody throws a bolt of taffeta at you."

Marcella started to speak but Eva Jo's raised hand stopped her.

"Dora Mae, honey, did it ever occur to you that there are times when that good-looking young preacher of yours takes that collar off? Or that maybe he doesn't even put it on unless he thinks he might run into you and you'd need his services?"

"I've seen him without that collar and black shirt. Hardly recognized him," Jewell said. "Glad I did, though. I was about to give him what for one day when he got my parking place at Lassiter's Laundromat."

"There's nothing in the play for anyone to be ashamed of, whoever they are," Marcella said. "And he won't be parking any cars."

Dora Mae patted her face. "My, my. Is my face red? It's burning up."

"Step in the kitchen and pour yourself a glass of iced tea. That'll fix you up," Eva Jo said.

CHAPTER THIRTY-ONE

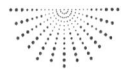

FRED STARNES AND JESSE MET LINDA CRUZ, GRUMPY, AND Jeremiah Downs in the church hall for the first rehearsal. It would be a read-through during which the three actors read their parts together from start to finish for the first time.

"I presume each of you have read through the script," Fred said. "Is there anyone who hasn't acquainted his or herself with the play?"

"I have," Linda said.

"So have I," Reverend Downs said.

"And you?" Fred said, directing his attention toward Grumpy.

"Yes, sir. I read it from one end to the other. Confused myself a time or two trying to keep it straight who was talking, but I done it."

"Great, now we'll begin. In our first reading I don't expect perfection, but I would like to get an idea how you think your characters would speak and emote," Fred said.

Grumpy raised his hand halfway. "I don't mind telling ya, Mr. Starnes."

"Fred will be fine," Fred said.

"Okay. I don't mind telling ya that I feel like a bull that got turned loose in a china closet. I can read and all, but sometimes big words kinda throw me off."

"That's fine," Fred said. "We can work through any problem words that come up."

"Okay, good. What's emote mean?"

Linda kindly defined the word for Grumpy.

"Funny how a guy can live his entire life and never hear a word," Grumpy said.

Jesse patted Grumpy on the back. "Don't worry about it. That happens to everyone."

They read through their lines with no intervention from Fred or Jesse.

"Very good," Fred said. "Let's do it again. This time try to express yourselves a little more as you read."

"Reverend Downs—"

"Jeremiah will be fine," the reverend said.

Jesse continued. "Jeremiah, perhaps you can demonstrate what Fred means as you read your lines."

For two more hours the five of them worked, laying the groundwork for what they hoped would turn into an enjoyable performance for their audience.

At Lucy's Cafe, Stella poured iced tea for Marcella and coffee for Edgar. "Now, what can I get you two for dinner?"

"We'll make it easy for you," Marcella said.

"We'd each like pot roast," Edgar said.

"Two pot roast dinners," Stella said. "How about the veggies? We've got the usuals, plus this evening we've got roasted asparagus, baby carrots, and mashed garlic cauliflower."

"Mashed cauliflower?" Marcella said.

"Who would have even thought Stella's Cafe in tiny little Morgan Crossroads, Alabama would ever serve something like that?" Stella said. "There was a nice couple stopped in here a couple weeks ago and asked for it. I told them I'd never heard of it, then stood there for a few minutes while they told me all about it. So here we are. Of course, you can still have our original lumpy mashed potatoes if you'd rather."

"Okay, Marcella will be the brave one," Edgar said, winking. "She can try the cauliflower and I'll stick with lumpy potatoes. She's more adventuresome than I."

"Garlic mashed cauliflower sounds wonderful to me," Marcella said, tossing a smile in Edgar's direction. "Stella, you choose the other vegetables. Surprise us."

"Okay, two surprise vegetables coming up," Stella said. "I'll be back with more tea and coffee."

The front door squeaked and the miniature cow bell rang when Eva Jo entered. She gravitated straight to Marcella.

"Hey, you two. Mind if I join you?"

Edgar half-stood, reaching to pull a chair out.

"Go on. Sit down and drink your coffee," Eva Jo said.

Stella spotted Eva Jo and started toward the table with a menu and a water pitcher.

Eva Jo held up her hand. "Don't bother with a menu. Just bring me whatever Marcella's having and a glass of sweet tea."

Stella soon appeared with three dinners. Edgar got his roast beef and lumpy mashed potatoes along with a surprise side of roasted asparagus. Marcella and Eva Jo each got pot roast, garlic mashed cauliflower with a side of steamed broccoli.

"I'll be back with your rolls," Stella said.

Eva Jo stared at her plate, glanced at Marcella's, then stared at Edgar's. "What's wrong with our potatoes?" Eva Jo asked.

"What potatoes?" Edgar asked, trying to hide a grin.

"These," Eva Jo said, pointing at the fluffy white delicacy on her plate and Marcella's. She dipped her nose near her plate. "Smells like garlic and parsley, and maybe something else. I can see a touch of black pepper in them and some butter, but they sure don't look like Edgar's. You don't reckon somebody fell asleep cooking these, do you?"

Marcella put her hand on Eva Jo's forearm. "Honey, those aren't lumpy potatoes."

"I can tell that," Eva Jo said. "Ain't a lump in whatever this stuff on my plate is. Those two grandsons of mine can't boil water without burning it, and I'm pretty sure they could do a better job mashing potatoes than this. I've told them over and over to leave some lumps in them. I'm surprised at Stella."

Stella overheard her name being mentioned and stepped over to Eva Jo. "Is something wrong?"

"Honey, you generally put out the best food anywhere around here, but in all the years I've been coming here, I've never got such sickly, watery looking potatoes as these. Are you feeling okay?"

Stella rested one hand on Marcella's shoulder and the other on Eva Jo's. "I'm fine. And those aren't potatoes."

Eva Jo snapped toward Marcella. "If that ain't potatoes, what in the blazes is it?"

"It's garlic mashed cauliflower," Stella said.

"It's what?" Eva Jo asked.

"Garlic mashed cauliflower," Marcella said. She took a bite, savored it for a moment and said. "It's delicious."

"Somebody tricked me," Eva Jo said.

"Now hold on," Stella said. "Remember, Edgar's an attorney. We can't have any false accusations."

"I never asked for cauliflower. In fact, you know I normally don't order anything I can't spell," Eva Jo said.

Edgar straightened himself. With a teasing air of solemnity, he said to Eva Jo, "Ma'am, I don't believe anyone has tricked you. You asked for the same that Marcella had ordered, but failed to ask what that was."

"Try them," Marcella said. "I bet they'll surprise you."

"Okay, but first, you try them," Eva Jo said, holding her plate toward Marcella.

Marcella dipped her unused salad fork into Eva Jo's cauliflower. "Stella, I believe her's may be even better than mine."

Eva Jo huffed and said, "Okay, okay. But next time–"

Stella patted Eva Jo on the back. "How about a round of hot fudge brownies and ice cream when you've finished, on the house?"

CHAPTER THIRTY-TWO

Henry carried a small table out to the porch at the general store and set up a mini-buffet of sourdough biscuits along with sausage, ham, and cheese to stuff in them. "There's coffee and orange juice on the counter inside. Help yourself and build your own biscuits."

It was less than a week until the big day. Ollie, Grumpy, Henry, and all the other men they could muster met on the porch. How could they transform Morgan Crossroads on fundraiser day from the sleepy little community it was to what they hoped would be the attraction of the year in that part of the state?

"Look here," Ollie said. "When we first came up with this harebrained idea we were just gonna have us a pretty good sized yard sale to pay for fixing up the park."

"I figure we can lay the blame on the ladies," Grumpy said.

"How do you reckon we can do that?" Henry said. "They knew nothing about it until we over-committed ourselves and had to recruit them to help us."

"Yes, but if you remember right, it was those women

cooking up whatever they were cooking up in that Rosebud Circle meeting that started us to thinking up our own to-do."

"Nobody's ever come right out and said it," Edgar said, holding a bitten biscuit up for display. "But I have a feeling that whole secret thing with the ladies was nothing more than them trying to find a beau for Linda Cruz."

"Did it work?" Michael Clomper asked.

"We don't know," Henry and Ollie said.

"Polly tells me that the big topic of discussion in the beauty shop is about you and Linda taking each other out to eat," Henry said.

"Yep, and my wife said she heard through somebody's grapevine that you and Miss Linda have been seen walking each other up and down Main Street in the evenings," Ollie said.

All eyes turned toward Michael.

"Well," Grumpy said through a bite of biscuit, "Did ya?"

Michael took a big swallow of orange juice just as the sausage fell out of his biscuit and landed on his boot. "Maybe."

"Go for it," Edgar said. "If she's the one for you, just go right on with it."

"You know what we used to say about such things back when we were kids," Ollie said.

"Some of us weren't around then," Jesse said. "What did you say?"

"I can't remember all of it, but it went sorta like this. Michael and Linda walking down the street, k-i-s-s-i-n-g," Ollie said in a rhythmic way, wagging his finger in time with the beat. "First comes love, then comes marriage. Then comes Michael with the baby carriage. Or something like that."

Michael bent to pick up the runaway sausage without looking at anyone.

"No need to blush, Michael," Grumpy said. "There's nobody here but us bunch of buffalo. Linda's a fine one. Ain't nobody here got anything sideways to say about that."

"That's right," Henry said. "You two just go on with whatever works out for you. You'll not hear any nonsense out of me."

Coffee cups and orange juice went up across the porch in a toast to Michael. "Cheers."

POLLY STOPPED MASSAGING SHAMPOO INTO ONE OF THE TWINS' hair and said, "I still haven't figured out how we got roped into working our tails off for a project the men started. Have any of you?"

"Well, they can be a bit helpless at times," Dora Mae said.

"How would you know anything about men?" Jewell asked. "It's not like you have a lifetime of experience living with them."

"Perhaps not, but never forget that I have the keen eye of a reporter."

"Except for the nosy part of your eye, you don't get much practice reporting about men around here," Eva Jo said.

"That's right. Gossiping and reporting aren't exactly the same thing, are they?" Jewell said.

"Not around here, they aren't," Eva Jo said. "But back to Polly's question, I think we got roped into it because we're here. I heard Ollie was about beside himself, trying to figure out how he'd gotten all his buddies in such a pickle."

"I think their idea just exploded into something bigger than they anticipated," Marcella said. "Don't take this for a fact, but I strongly suspect that they were trying to get one up on us ladies and it just got out of hand."

"I think you're right," Jewell said, pouring herself a cup of coffee. "First, they said they were going to clean up the old park, and then before they knew it they had collected a barn full of stuff for a yard sale. But they had no way to bring people up in this valley to buy any of it."

Eva Jo bolted out of her chair. The other twin jerked her purse up off the floor, expecting an emergency run for the door.

"Has anybody made signs to put up on the highway?" Eva Jo asked. "I haven't heard a word about any signs or ads on the radio. How do they think anybody's going to know about all this?"

"They've only got three days," Polly said.

"We mustn't let them know that we think they forgot something that important," Marcella said. "I'll ask Edgar if they need help distributing the signs."

"Tell him I'll help if they need me," Jewell said.

"A dollar to a hole in a donut says they forgot to order signs," Eva Jo said. "Michael sure hasn't said anything about them."

"I should put that in *The Whipper County Gazette*," Dora Mae said.

"That's a step in the right direction," Eva Jo said. "But nobody reads it outside Morgan Crossroads, and we already know about it."

CHAPTER THIRTY-THREE

THE NEXT MORNING OLLIE DROVE HIS FLATBED FARM TRUCK TO Brown's General Store where he met Henry, Grumpy, and Michael promptly at eight o'clock.

Marcella had phoned acquaintances at several area churches and asked to borrow folding tables for the yard sale.

After two cups of coffee and a honey bun, Ollie left with Grumpy to collect tables from the Methodist church in Gurley, the Holiness church down by the creek, and the Presbyterian church over at the foot of the mountain. Henry and Michael headed for Porterville to gather tables from the Church of Christ, then the other direction to the little Baptist church at the top of the mountain.

A dozen volunteers from neighboring communities joined the two teams posting signs that Edgar had purchased on fence posts, store windows, and any other place where they might be seen by passersby. By the time they returned to the general store, the entire valley, and the outlying areas had been well marked with invitations to attend the yard sale. Signs dotted the roadside from Rainsville on Sand

Mountain to the Huntsville city limit and from Guntersville north to Huntland across the state line in Tennessee. "Community-wide yard sale," they announced in large red letters. Across the bottom of each sign were the words, "Live performance of *An Evening in April*, the best play you've never seen."

Other men helped set the tables up around Morgan Crossroads, most within two or three blocks of the light at the intersection of the Porterville highway and Main Street. By mid-afternoon there were seventy-five tables planted in yards, along sidewalks, in parking lots. Wherever there was space for it, there was a table.

Eva Jo contributed the use of her tractor and bush hog to cut the over-grown grass at the park, transforming it into a make-shift parking lot. They set portable concession stands up in four places. The stands were borrowed from the school in Porterville and the fairground in the next county.

Fred Starnes, Jesse, and Pastor Jeremiah Downs had their hands full making final adjustments to the set arrangements on the stage in Morgan Chapel. They tested and retested the stage lighting. Michael Clomper opened and closed the curtains across both halves of the stage several times for assurance.

Dora Mae Crawford tore herself away from her role of reporter/editor long enough to vacuum the carpet and dust the furnishings in the sanctuary turned theater.

Polly and the twins made sure the costumes were ironed and hung in order, according to the list that Fred Starnes had provided them.

East of town on her farm, Eva Jo baked furiously. Linda Cruz arranged cakes, muffins, and cookies on cooling racks around the kitchen. Sheet pans of uncut fudge and divinity candy sat on top of the large chest freezer. Liz Farrel from the bakery in Porterville stopped by with several dozen donuts she'd donated.

According to the weather reports on the Huntsville television stations, there would be beautiful weather for the next few days.

Marcella phoned the women and Henry phoned the men. Everyone involved in the festivities was asked to meet at Lucy's Cafe at six o'clock for a final strategy meeting, and the only joint meeting. That included the crew for the yard sale and the concessions people. Fred Starnes and his group would be there.

Marcella called ahead and asked Stella if, rather than taking orders for the entire crowd at once, she might just serve everyone buffet style. Pay one price. Eat as much as you want. Free sweet tea refills, as usual.

After dinner, Henry stood. Adjusting the straps on his overalls, he said, "I'm not sure if any of us ever thought we'd see this day. Seems like it's been years since Ollie first came up with the idea for a fundraiser. It's only been a few months, though, and here we are, just a few hours away from the biggest yard sale this area's ever seen." Henry raised his tea glass to Fred Starnes. "And thanks to our friend here, Mr. Starnes, we're going to put on the only real play that's ever been done in this valley."

Dora Mae stood and clapped, then Linda Cruz. Everyone else except Fred Starnes followed. He raised his hand shyly in acceptance and mouthed a thank you.

"Ollie's the guy who's going to supervise setting up the yard sale," Henry said, ceding the floor to Ollie.

"I'm guessing you all have figured out that it's gonna be a short night for most of us. My grandson talked the fellows on his football team over at the high school into helping us take the stuff from my barn and cart it around to all the tables. Grumpy's gonna drive one truck and Henry's gonna drive the other one."

"I'm glad the boys are going to help, but who's going to arrange the stuff so it looks presentable?" Polly asked.

"We can help with that," one twin said. The other twin nodded.

"Don't forget, now. There's something like six dozen tables scattered around that have to be loaded with knick-knacks and such," Grumpy said.

"Ouch," Eva Jo said.

"I can help set up the sale tables," Jewell Crabtree said.

"If my hunch is right, we'll see people coming into town before breakfast," Ollie said. "If they're anything like my wife is when she gets in a mood for yardsaling, they'll be here about five minutes after the sun wakes up." He looked at Polly next to him and winked.

"Well, we'd best get on with it, then," Eva Jo said. "By the time we get all that stuff spread out and covered up against the dew, it'll be time to wake up again."

With that, people slid away from their tables and the collective scraping and clanging of chair legs signaled the beginning of the day everyone had been anxious to see.

CHAPTER THIRTY-FOUR

THE FIRST CAR STOPPED IN FRONT OF LUCY'S CAFE AT 4:11 a.m., just minutes after the lights went on across the intersection at Brown's General Store.

Henry squinted through the store window toward the unknown car, then looked at his watch. A twinge of nervousness zigged and zagged through his body.

Another vehicle, which Henry recognized from a distance to be Grumpy's, rattled into sight and stopped in the lot next to the store.

"We might better get started," Grumpy said. "Where's everybody else?"

"They'll be here soon," Henry said as a car from Georgia pulled in next to the store. "At least, they'd better be. Get on the phone, Grumpy. Call the others and tell them to get their behinds up here."

Within ten minutes, there was more traffic passing under the light than there'd been at shift change time when the rug factory was still in business.

Eva Jo and Michael roared into Lucy's Cafe's parking lot. Michael helped his granny carry the trays of various small breakfast biscuits and fruit inside where the women were to meet. Then he carried a large roasting pan full of bulging biscuits and muffins across the intersection to the general store for the men.

"Lord, would you look out there?" Eva Jo said.

Polly and Marcella walked to the window and followed Eva Jo's suggestion.

"Where are all these people coming from?" Polly asked.

"All over, I'd say," Marcella said. "Edgar ordered several hundred signs, and they were all posted somewhere across the area. I think there may be a notice in the Scottsboro paper, too."

"How much did you say this set of salt and peppers shakers was?" asked a hefty woman with an accent that appeared to have originated somewhere north of the Mason Dixon line.

"Let's see here," one twin said, taking the shakers in hand. "Five dollars. Can I bag them up for you?"

"Seventy-five cents," the lady replied.

"They're five dollars," said the second twin.

At the next table, the twins heard the same unmistakable voice uttering "a dollar fifty" for a large metal box full of hand tools. When she went out of site, she was still empty-handed.

A white-haired lady with a cane nudged up to the table of salt and pepper shakers and admired the sizable collection. She picked up the same pair as the lady with the accent and turned them bottom side up to read the price tag. She whispered to the man who appeared to be her other and considerably older half.

"Miss, I see a five dollar tag on this set. How many pairs are there in total?"

"Oh my," the first twin said with a hand on her cheek.

"A bunch," said the second twin. "We have these, plus all those on that other table behind you."

The lady's husband steadied her as she pivoted for a look behind her. Her eyes widened and a smile crossed her face. "Would you take four dollars per pair if we bought the entire group?"

The twins looked at each other, not sure if they were authorized to make such a deal. The second twin said, "Yes, Ma'am, we can do that. We'll help you pack them."

The lady hugged her husband and wiped away an escaped tear. "I had a collection of more than a thousand pairs, but lost them in a house fire two years ago."

The twins summoned help from a neighboring table and together they and the purchasing couple wrapped more than a thousand pairs of salt and pepper shakers, most of them old and rare. They accepted part of the payment in cash and with Ollie's permission, a check for the rest.

Dave Crabtree helped the couple take their purchase to their car. When he returned to the now empty table, he said to the twins, "That wife of mine is never gonna let me live this one down."

"Live what down?" asked the first twin.

"Four dollars a pair for the bunch. Those shakers were Jewell's, and we did all kinds of arguing about them over the years. She tried to tell me some of them were worth a bunch of money to the right person. I told her there wasn't a breathing soul that would give her more than fifty cents for them."

"Well, there's about four thousand dollars in that cash box that wasn't there a few minutes ago," the second twin said.

NOBODY IN THEIR MOST POSITIVE FRAME OF MIND EVER imagined the crowd that wiggled and waggled its way through Morgan Crossroads, Alabama that day.

As Morgan Crossroads's unofficial and unpaid overseer, Cecil Grey phoned two neighboring counties asking them to loan sheriff deputies. Each agreed to send one. The state of Alabama dispatched a trooper. Four off-duty policemen from nearby towns volunteered for traffic duty.

Marcella and Edgar had been inside the church with Fred Starnes for most of the morning. They had not seen just how many people there were until Edgar opened the door on his way to Lucy's for box lunches.

"Marcella. Fred. Come look at Morgan Crossroads," Edgar said.

Fred was speechless. Marcella lit up. Edgar looked across toward Lucy's Cafe and saw that the street had disappeared from view.

"Marcella! Mr. Starnes!" Dora Mae Crawford's voice was coming from somewhere, but Marcella couldn't tell quite where. "Edgar, over here!"

Edgar spotted a hand with a white glove waving just above the shoulders of two men near the sidewalk. He caught just enough eye contact that Dora Mae stopped yelling and ducked around the two men on her way to the church door.

"What is it?" Marcella asked the out of breath Dora Mae.

"We, we ... we have ..."

Edgar laid his hand lightly on Dora Mae's shoulder. "Take a breath, Dora Mae."

"Is there a problem?" Fred Starnes asked.

"Big problem," Dora Mae gasped, holding her hands wide apart.

"Okay, honey, I'm sure it's manageable," Marcella said. "What's the problem?"

"Ticket sales," Dora Mae said. "They're not going at all like we planned."

Fred Starnes's shoulders fell. "What do you mean? Aren't tickets selling at all?"

"Oh, yes. Yes, they are. How many seats are in the sanctuary?"

"Dora Mae, you're there almost every Sunday," Marcella said.

"I know, but I've never counted the seating positions."

"We can seat two hundred fifty. I'd be thrilled if we could fill even half of those," Fred said.

"Well, Eva Jo said this is either going to make you glad or mad, but we've sold eight hundred tickets."

"Eight hundred!" Edgar said, looking at Marcella, then Fred, and back at Dora Mae.

"Miss Crawford," Fred said.

"Dora Mae, please," Dora Mae half-whispered.

Fred continued. "Miss Crawford, did you say eight hundred?"

Edgar relaxed and looked down into Dora Mae's eyes. "How did you sell so many tickets? I assume you were counting as you sold, weren't you?"

"Not exactly," Dora Mae said to the rose bush beside Edgar. "You gave me that big ole roll of tickets and I just took ten dollars apiece for them until suddenly, they were gone. I was so excited. I just forgot all about counting them. Maybe you should have just given me 250 to sell."

Marcella looked at Edgar with a raised eyebrow that hinted Dora Mae might have a point. "Where are we going to seat that many people?"

Eva Jo rounded the corner of the building carrying a bag

and a small cooler. "Lunch time, people. Save you having to walk across the street."

"Eva Jo, where are we going to seat eight hundred people on such short notice?" Marcella asked.

Eva Jo nodded toward Dora Mae. "Ask her. I've got no dog in this hunt." She pulled out a sandwich piled high with deli style ham, a bag of chips, and a Double Cola for each person.

Fred hesitated a moment with a puzzled look on his face. "A dog in this hunt?"

"She's claiming immunity," Dora Mae said without looking at him.

"I told her she was losing count," Eva Jo said. "That hard little head of hers wouldn't listen to me until she ran out of tickets and I threatened to force-feed her a jar of sour pickles if she didn't count the stubs."

Edgar held both hands up, palms out as if he were about to part the Red Sea. "You've collected ten dollars each for eight hundred tickets. Is that right, Dora Mae?"

"Yes. Ten dollars apiece for all of them."

"Okay. Then I'd say we have two choices. Either present the play three times this evening, or prepare ourselves to refund a lot of money to a lot of unhappy people."

"Can we present the play three times?" Marcella asked, looking at Fred Starnes.

"Yes, we can do that, given enough time between each to reset the stage, and assuming the actors and stagehands are up to it."

"Unless my addition and subtraction has gone all rusty, it looks to me like we're still gonna have about fifty people that can't get in," Eva Jo said.

"Raise the windows and let some of them look in from

outside," Dora Mae said. "Those windows aren't painted shut are they?"

"They might be right now, but we can get them open somehow between now and then if the preacher's okay with it," Eva Jo said, chuckling and pulling Dora Mae into a hug. "If he's not, Dora Mae can be the one to tell the last fifty they ain't gettin' in."

CHAPTER THIRTY-FIVE

OLLIE AND HENRY LEANED ON THE PORCH RAIL AT BROWN'S General Store taking a breather.

"Look out across there," Ollie said. "Did you ever in your life think so many folks would come through Morgan Crossroads at one time?"

"You kiddin'? I'm not so sure there's been this many in the whole history of this place. Looks like a county fair, doesn't it?"

Ollie took a swallow of his RC Cola. "How come we didn't think about that? We could've talked to somebody about setting up some carnival rides over there in the park."

"I suppose we could've done that, but then, where would we put all these cars? If we hadn't had that park area available, people would have been lined up half-way to Porterville trying to get in."

The air reminded Henry and Ollie of July 4th or Memorial Day, when people fire up grills in half the backyards in Morgan Crossroads. At all four concession stands volunteers manned a grill, sending out burgers and hotdogs as fast as they could cook them.

"This was a pretty decent idea you had, Ollie, even if it did sound a little harebrained at first. I'd say we're going to be able to fix that park up real nice," Henry said. "Say, did Edgar tell you he sold some of that antique furniture to somebody in Huntsville? Got a good price for it, too."

"Well, there you go. It's looking better all the time," Ollie said. He'd already told Henry about the salt and pepper shaker sale and through the grapevine they'd heard about Dora Mae's overly zealous turn as ticket seller. More than half the tables were empty, their wares gone to locals and tourists from several states, if the out-of-state car tags meant anything.

"Hey, Henry. Ollie." Linda Cruz hurried by, summoned to the church-turned-theater.

Henry and Ollie threw up their hands.

"You reckon Michael Clomper's ever gonna get that girl under his spell?" Ollie said.

"I don't know. But if he doesn't, he's sure gonna be missing out on a fine young lady."

Jeremiah Downs hurried behind Linda, apparently a recipient of the same "get here right now" message. He threw his hand up and yelled over his shoulder, "See you after the play."

"There goes Michael's competition," Ollie said.

Henry flicked a toothpick into the gravel. "You think so?"

"I've heard a dozen people say that young preacher man ain't interested in gettin' married, but I don't know. His ears kinda perk up a bit every time he gets around her."

"Maybe," Henry said. "I've seen Michael get all fumble fingered and acting like he can't talk straight when she comes within ten yards of him, but I've never noticed anything like that with the preacher."

Henry and Ollie walked down the middle of Main Street, waving, grunting howdies, and taking in the noise.

Polly ran up behind Henry. "Where's Grumpy?"

"No idea. Have you looked in the church? We saw Linda Cruz and the preacher hot-footing it over there."

"Well, Marcella's trying to find him. If you see him, tell him he's gonna miss out on his chance at Hollywood if he doesn't show up pretty quick."

Just past the next concession stand, there sat Grumpy on a bench devouring what appeared to be his third hotdog, judging by the empty wrappers in his lap.

"It's show time," Ollie said.

Grumpy pulled the stop watch out of his overall bib pocket. "Not yet. Still got two hours."

"No, sir. That's the old schedule."

Grumpy's brow raised into a ragged arch. "What's that mean?"

Henry nudged him on the shoulder. "That means you'd better get the lead out. Everybody's waiting on you over at the church."

"Why are they waiting on me?"

Ollie took the hotdog wrappers from Grumpy. "Some time tomorrow you can thank Dora Mae for overselling the place by a few hundred seats."

"How'd she do that?" Grumpy said, ramping up to a near trot.

"Ask Eva Jo," Ollie yelled. "Dora Mae's too busy scraping windows to stop and visit with you."

———

MICHAEL CLOMPER HAD PRACTICED HIS TIMING OPENING AND closing the curtains but was running through it just a couple more times before the door opened for the recently decided three o'clock performance. *Not too fast. Not too slow.* Let the curtains open and close without swaying too much.

Mary Beth was charged with the wardrobe and costume changes and was busy straightening Jeremiah Downs's shirt.

With the curtain closed, Linda Cruz ran through her lines. From stage right, Michael watched her, oblivious to anyone else's whereabouts.

Behind him, Eva Jo watched, but said nothing for a moment. In a calm, quiet voice that Michael rarely heard from his grandmother, she said, "You wondering what it might've been like to play Jeremiah Downs's part?"

Snatched out of his daydream, Michael said, "How long have you been standing there?"

"Just a couple minutes, that's all. So, how about it? You dreaming a little bit?"

"Maybe."

"Are you worried the preacher's gonna nab her when all this is over?"

Michael waved the idea away. "No! Well, maybe."

"What if tonight goes away like it never happened and the preacher goes back to preaching and Linda goes back to filling prescriptions?"

"Granny, if I tell you something, can you keep it a secret?"

"Of course, I can. What do you think I am?"

"Well, from the time I was in grade school, I heard kids say you were the root of the grapevine around here. I never knew what they meant until I was grown."

"Is that what you think? Do you think you can't trust me enough to tell me when you're squeezed up a little inside or maybe you're in love for the first time?"

"No, I don't really think that. You never told Dad it was

me that backed your tractor into his truck. He always said he couldn't understand how you did that."

"Well, no, I never told him. Lord knows he backed into enough stuff on his own."

"Granny, Linda Cruz is the prettiest girl I've ever known."

"Yep," Eva Jo said. "She is way up yonder above the average in looks. And she's smart, too. Have you ever told her that?"

"No. She might think I was coming on to her or something like that.

"Well, I'd say that's a mark or two in your favor, and hers, too."

"What's that supposed to mean?"

"That means she's paid enough attention to you that she's coming to know you. And as for the coming on part, that just tells me you care what she thinks. That's more than I can say about any of my husbands."

IMMACULATELY DRESSED, FRED STARNES STEPPED INTO THE pastor's office, turned green room. "Show time!"

Within two minutes, everyone was in place.

The sanctuary was full. Outside, at least three people stood at each window.

Edgar straightened his tie and took one last glance at his shoes, then walked onstage. Applause and whistles rose across the room. He raised his hand to usher in silence.

"Ladies and gentlemen, welcome to the world's first performance of a play written and directed by Mr. Fred Starnes from Los Angeles, California. Our cast includes Miss Linda Cruz as Gwendolyn, Mr. Jeremiah Downs as Peter, and our very own Grumpy as the uncle and neighbor, Mr.

Fishborn. Please hold your applause until the end. I give you *An Evening In April.*"

The curtain opened to a beautifully designed set and lighting that was as good as it could have been with the windows open on a sunny Saturday.

Mr. Fishborn and Peter sat at a breakfast table discussing the news they'd heard on the radio that a gardener in New England had wooed a wealthy lady from San Francisco into marriage.

"I heard he convinced her to marry him by promising her a garden of tulips and forsythia," Peter said.

"I can't imagine the work it would take to create such a garden," Mr. Fishborn said.

Through a door near the table Gwendolyn entered, well dressed.

Peter stood to greet her. "My dear, you look marvelous in that dress."

"Gwendolyn would be right cute—I meant to say, she'd look marvelous in any dress," Mr. Fishborn said, hoping no one had caught his blunder. Hushed chuckles across the audience indicated that he'd lost his wish.

"Why, thank you, Mr. Fishborn. That's very kind of you," Gwendolyn said just before she kissed Peter on the cheek.

Peter stood and returned the kiss, kicking the table leg in the process. "Did you hear the story Mr. Fishborn told about the gardener who promised a garden if a certain lady would marry him?"

"No, I haven't heard that one." She turned to Mr. Fishborn. "Tell me the story, please."

Mr. Fishborn retold the story with interjections by Peter.

"If the right man were to make me such a promise, I might reconsider my vow to remain single," Gwendolyn said, tilting her head toward Peter.

To the scratchy sounds of a Victrola in the background, Gwendolyn and Peter swept their way across the stage and back in a fluid-like dance.

Forty-five minutes and two set changes later curtains closed to roaring applause on the first performance of the play. Allowing forty-five minutes between each to reset props and change audiences, they performed *An Evening In April* two more times to overwhelming acceptance.

Following each performance, the cast took their bows. After the last performance, the cast asked Fred Starnes to join them after the bow. At the end of a short story telling how the play had been written decades earlier and hidden in a box, it was as if the applause and whistling might lift the entire Morgan Chapel roof off the building.

For the first time, Fred Starnes allowed a smile to cross his face.

After the crowd had disbursed and the work of clearing the props from the sanctuary for the next day's Sunday service had been done, Michael Clomper caught up with Linda Cruz.

"You were amazing tonight."

"Thank you," Linda said. "That's sweet of you."

Shuffling, he said, "I'm serious. You know that part in the beginning about the guy offering to plant that lady a garden if she'd marry him?"

Linda slowly lifted her eyes to meet his. "Yes," she said, dragging the word out.

"Well, I would plant you an entire field of whatever flower you wanted if I thought I had any chance at all of marrying you." He focused on her eyes and hoped she didn't notice the tremble in his hands.

She hesitated, then smiled and said, "Let me think about it. They'd have to be flowers that bloomed in April."

CHAPTER THIRTY-SIX

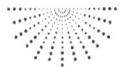

The Whipper County Gazette
Special Edition
Dora Mae Crawford, Editor-in-Chief

YESTERDAY, MORGAN CROSSROADS, ALABAMA WAS A NEW community to me. I've never seen so many people from so many places wadded into our little town. In case any of my readers missed the news, we had a fundraiser to help pay for fixing up the park.

There was a huge yard sale and toward the end of the day, a beautiful theatrical performance for everyone to enjoy. It was my first play to attend as an adult. Personally, I don't see how that Shakespeare fellow could have done any better.

From what I hear, we may be able to fix up more than the park.

I've always worked hard to put out a newspaper that just told things like they were, or at least how they appeared to me. Sometimes people didn't think too much of me for that.

And sometimes, I might not have been too nice to certain people, and people weren't too fond of me for that, either.

One of the people who may not have seen my nicer side was Fred Starnes, who has been staying with Marcella and Edgar Garrison for a while. He is the man who wrote the play and promised to stay around here until he had directed the live performances.

Mister Starnes, I, for one, hope you don't leave and go back to California. You've found yourself a family around here if you want it to be that way. We could stand a little extra class around here from time to time—not that Marcella and Edgar don't have their own class. I'm sure everyone in Morgan Crossroads feels the same.

Just one last thing, Mister Starnes. It would be wrong of me if I didn't say that I was sorry for talking ugly about you. You're not uppity. You're just different enough from most of us that we might be able to learn a thing or two from you.

Welcome back, Mister Starnes.

IF YOU ENJOYED WELCOME BACK MISTER STARNES

Please consider returning to the online store where you purchase books and leave an honest review. Your review will help other readers find this book and the Morgan Crossroads Series of fun fiction.

ABOUT THE AUTHOR

Tom Buford is an author of fun small town and rural fiction for the entire family. He and his bride have been married more than 47 years and make their home in rural Tennessee.

You can learn more about Tom and his writing on his website at:

TomBuford.com

Be sure to register for Tom's mailing list to keep up to date with Marcella, Eva Jo, Dora Mae, and the rest of Morgan Crossroads.

TomBuford.com/subscribe

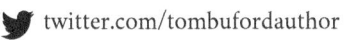 twitter.com/tombufordauthor
 pinterest.com/tombufordauthor
 goodreads.com/TomBuford

ALSO BY TOM BUFORD

Long Time Coming

Living With Fibromyalgia Patients: 79 Ways You Can Make Their Lives Better